KING'S

The KING Trilogy

Book One

Mimi Jean Pamfiloff

OTHER WORK BY MIMI JEAN PAMFILOFF

KING FOR A DAY
(Book 2, The King Trilogy)

FATE BOOK (a New Adult Novel)

The Accidentally Yours Series

Accidentally in Love with…a God?
Accidentally Married to…a Vampire?
Sun God Seeks…Surrogate?
Accidentally…Evil? (a Novella)
Vampires Need Not…Apply?
Accidentally…Cimil? (a Novella)
Accidentally…Over? (Series Finale)
AUGUST 2014

COMING JULY 2014

Happy Pants Café
(a Contemporary Romance Series)

COMING LATE 2014

KING OF ME (Book 3, the King Trilogy)
FATE BOOK 2 (a New Adult Novel)

DEDICATED TO
MY STREET TEAM

For giving me something to laugh about or drool over every day. You kinky f***ing ladies rock!

Ale, Ally, Amy, Ann, Annette, Ashlee, Ashley H., Ashley L., Bethany, Blythe, Bridget, Cathy S., Cathy S. L., Ces, Christina, Courtney, Dalitza, Dy, Farah, Hannah, Helen, Hida, Ingrid, Ixtzel, Janna, Jean, Jennifer B., Jennifer D, Jessa (our leader!), Jodian (#farmerunicorns), Kassie B., Kim K., Kim M., Kim M. (again), Kirsty, Leah, Lindsay, Mai Ling, Mary, Marybell, Michaela, Nadine, Nikki, Reagan, Shana-kay, Shasta, Sofia, Sonya, Terri, Tina, Vicki (woof!), Vickie, and…deep breath, can't believe I made it to the end of the list…Wanda!

CHAPTER ONE

San Francisco.
Present Day. 5:57 P.M.

I squirmed in my tight gray pencil-skirt from behind the antique desk and forced myself to look away.

Three minutes to go.

But I didn't need a clock to tell me that. I knew it. My stomach knew it. And the sweat trickling down the small of my back beneath my fitted white blouse knew it.

Focus on something else, Mia.

I glanced at the drizzle of rain collecting outside on the office window, but I couldn't see past the film of dirt. Even if I could, I wouldn't see clouds or the long-overdue rain. I would only see *him*. Or, really, the mental ghost of his tailored black suit, jet black hair, and pale gray eyes powering through me from the darkened doorway, cautioning me not to speak. That was how he greeted me each evening before he walked directly to his private office and shut the door, leaving behind a subtle trail of delicious cologne. There would be no other exchange between us. His cologne. My nose. Oh yes, I almost forgot. The phone calls.

At exactly 6:02 p.m., he would call my desk, a mere five feet from his door, and say in that deep, mesmerizing voice that sent prickly chills to my bones, "That will be all, Miss Turner."

Those five feet felt like a thousand miles of scorching desert. One I dared not cross. Because while some people might be fooled by the exquisite lines of his handsome face or by his European arrogance that reeked of old money, I was not. I saw right through that rapturous smile. He was a cruel, sadistic son of a bitch. That was the only explanation as to why he kept me waiting like this, day after agonizing day, forcing me to swallow back my bile while the clock ticked away, all sense of hope dying with every breath I took.

I glanced at the clock once again.

One minute to go.

I continued reminding myself that I had to be strong this time—no getting tongue-tied or woozy—and demand what was mine. We had a deal. I wanted his help, he wanted…well, me. As his assistant. Only I just sat there like his personal museum piece. 6:00 a.m. to 6:02 p.m. Six days a week. On the sixth floor.

The devil likes sixes, I thought, *so why wouldn't this guy?*

What my new employer didn't like, however, were questions. "Just do, Miss Turner. Just do," he'd say.

"But do what?" I would ask.

Then he'd laugh, causing deep creases to form on both sides of his wickedly beautiful mouth. "As you are told, Miss Turner. As you are told," he'd say while his hypnotic, cold gaze said something else: *I own you now. Don't you ever fucking forget it.*

Maybe he was right. Maybe he did own me. I didn't know anymore. I just knew that I'd given up regretting the choice I'd made on that horrible, dark and rainy night when I'd come to him, crawling on hands and knees, praying he'd be the miracle I needed. But from the first moment he saw me, he was like a shark that tasted blood. Only, it was my desperation and weakness that had him salivating. And the things he did to me over this very desk I now sat at…*Oh Lord, I can't bear to think about it.* I should have turned around and run when I had the chance. Instead, I told myself that whatever it took, whatever the price, it was worth it. If he were the goddamned devil himself, it didn't matter. Just as long as he helped me.

But that was three long weeks ago, and my decision to make a deal with this evil man had bought me nothing but more time to think. Mostly about my fears. Fears I now knew inside and out. Fears that pecked away at the flesh of my soul like hell's vultures while I sat in a giant empty loft that no one ever visited, with a phone that never rang. Except when he called.

The clock on the wall struck six. The witching hour.

My gaze focused on the doorway, and I willed my unsteady nerves not to feel, not to be awestruck by the tall, supremely masculine figure I expected to find.

Empty.

I glanced down at my wristwatch, then back at the doorway. Where was he? I pulled a sharpened pencil from the holder—the only other thing on my desk aside from the phone and lamp—and began flicking the unused eraser against my palm.

6:01. My pulse accelerated.

He'd never been late. Not once. Had the evil bastard skipped town without holding up his end of the bargain? It's not like there was anything in this office he couldn't leave behind: two desks, two chairs, and two brass lamps. No computers. No mail. No clients. It was unsettling.

"Son of a bitch," I whispered. *We had a deal.*

I stared at the goddamned door, willing the sharp angles of his cheeks and his square, broad shoulders to darken it.

Nothing.

I glanced one last time at the clock.

6:02.

The phone on my lonely desk rang, jolting me in my chair.

Crap.

My hand shook as I reached for it. "He—hello?"

"It is time, Miss Turner."

"King?"

"No. It's your fucking fairy godmother, Miss Turner. And your wish has been granted."

I was speechless. Not because of what he said, but because his voice had such a crippling effect on me. In a million years, I'd never be able to articulate how he so rigidly divided my mind from my body. Hate and desire. My two halves sickened by each other.

"Miss Turner?"

I opened my mouth, but nothing came out.

"As usual, Miss Turner, I find myself questioning the value of our arrangement. One would expect his assistant to possess the ability to speak, at the very fucking least."

I wanted to tell him that he was the devil. The *goddamned* devil. Instead, I eked out two tiny words. Two words that I instantly despised myself for saying. They were weak. They were submissive. They were the last things on my mind, yet I said them anyway. "Thank you."

He laughed, sounding all too pleased. "Be at the airport with your passport in two hours. I'll email you the itinerary."

I wanted to ask where we were going, but knew better; he didn't like questions, and he was giving me what I wanted: help. At least, I hoped.

"And Miss Turner?" he added.

"Ye—yes?"

"Pack light. None of those fucking useless heels. Where we're going, you'll only need your wits. Anything else is just dead weight."

The phone clicked.

"King?"

The angry sound of a busy signal poured through the receiver.

Once again, I found myself wondering who I'd gotten myself mixed up with.

He's the man who can find anything, Mia. Anything. For a price.

If that was the case, would he find the one thing in this world I couldn't live without that had been taken from me?

I'd never know if I didn't go.

࿐

Four Weeks Earlier.
San Francisco.

"Honey, you look a little...pale," said my mother. Her powder-blue eyes, eyes much like my own, narrowed with suspicion from across my breakfast table. "You're not coming down with that flu, are you? It's going around."

"Fall is always the worst time of year," added my father, a retired school principal who now spent his days playing golf, fishing, and talking about random, meaningless crap he saw on the news.

"They have fifteen new strains already. Fifteen. And none of them are covered by the flu shot."

"Makes me wonder why we get one every year," my mother commented as she took a bite of her bagel, our usual Sunday brunch. Although they lived only five blocks away on Nob Hill in a renovated Victorian that had been in the family for over a hundred years, we didn't see each other much. My advertising job as a Global Campaign Manager kept me on the road a lot.

"Yeah. Makes you wonder," I added absently, sipping my coffee, a cold sweat building on my brow.

My father went on to talk about the fascinating process for deciding which viruses were picked to be the lucky winners each year or something like that. I stopped listening after the first ten words because my mind was preoccupied with something unimaginably horrific that I'd learned only three minutes prior to my parents' arrival. Something that would devastate them like it had just devastated me.

Kidnapped…How am I going to tell my parents?

You're not. This can't be real.

Besides, who would want to take Justin? My baby brother was the nicest guy on the planet. Ever. He was the sort of person who'd pick up worms off the sidewalk after a good rain and put them somewhere safe.

Who would want to harm him? Justin, of all people?

It wasn't like Justin and his team were digging up gold treasures down in Mexico; they were excavating ancient pots and plates—crap like that. I remember how excited he was when he'd found a pre-Hispanic button. But were those worth his life?

He's not dead, Mia. Not yet.

"Honey?" my mother asked. "Mia." She snapped her fingers and then looked at my father. "I think that blonde hair has gotten to her head."

I'd just had my wavy locks colored and then cut into a shoulder-length A-line bob the week before. It was practically the same shade I'd always had, just with a few highlights. The woman at the salon told me it would make my blue eyes pop. Not true. But I remember telling Justin about it. That was the last time we spoke.

Fuck. How? How can this be happening?

I blinked and lifted my head. "I'm going to Mexico to see Justin for a few weeks."

"Oh." My mom's opportunistic eyes lit up. "That's wonderful! You haven't had a vacation in years. But I thought you were due in New York tomorrow."

"Change of plans," I explained. "Spur of the moment thing. Completely forgot to tell you."

"Fantastic!" she said. "I'll run home and bring you the care package I was about to mail off. I got him all of his favorite seaweed treats and those socks he loves. You have room in your luggage, right?"

I nodded and faked a smile. "Sure. Plenty of room."

My father was silent for a few moments. "Mia, I know you're a world traveler, one of those jet-setters…"

Jet-setter? Did people even use that term anymore? I didn't know.

"But," he continued, "you should be careful. That place is dangerous. All those *bandidos* kidnapping people. And do you have any idea how many murders there are every year?"

Over thirty-one thousand. At least, that's what the Internet said. In any case, was Justin now one of them? Or did he fall into that other category? The *narcos* kidnapped people all the time to supplement their incomes.

"Oh, honey," my mother swatted my father's arm, "don't scare Mia. I'm sure she'll be fine. Besides, she'll be with Justin. Won't you, honey?" Justin was twenty-five, a year younger than me, but he was a big guy, just like my dad.

"Sure. I'll be with him the entire time," I lied.

My father leaned back in the chair, disapproval flickering in his green eyes, the same color eyes as Justin's. I wanted to scream. "Just be careful, Mia."

I took a breath, barely able to hold my composure. "I'll be fine, Dad. I promise." But I wouldn't be fine, and neither would they.

"Oh! I wish I could go with you! I'm dying to see Palenque." My mother paused. "You'll be back in time for my birthday, right? We're having a crab feed right on the pier."

I smiled and grabbed her hand. "Wouldn't miss it, Mom."

But that would become just another lie in a string of many to come, because our lives would never be the same.

CHAPTER TWO

When I'd received the phone call from the U.S. Embassy in Mexico City informing me that my brother and his team had been kidnapped from their archaeological dig site near Palenque, I had the distinct impression I was being sold a barrel of bullshit. After all, I was in advertising. I could smell bullshit from a mile away. The woman from the embassy assured me that the local police were doing everything they could to find the people who'd taken the team, but when she insisted there was no need for me to come to Mexico, my mind tripped. I felt like she was trying to keep me away. That's why I had to go.

After I got rid of my parents with some excuse of needing to run errands before the trip, I rang back the embassy. I couldn't remember her name, but I'd never forget her sticky sweet, bullshit voice. When I told her I was coming to Mexico to see her, she immediately pushed back.

"I can't just stay here doing nothing," I told her.

"Ma'am, we realize how traumatic this must be, but we advise the families of victims to stay home and focus on supporting each other. Let us work with the Mexican authorities."

"He's my brother, and I'm not asking permission. I *will* be involved."

There was a long pause, then a crackle on the other end of the phone. Was she eating a snack? "If you choose to come, we cannot stop you." She crunched down on whatever she was eating. "We simply ask that you do not impede the investigation."

Why would I want to impede anyone from finding my brother?

"Just tell me who to ask for when I get there," I said.

I heard the sound of more crunching. *Heartless bitch.*

"You can ask for me, Jamie Henshaw."

I scribbled down her name, holding back a terrible scream. "Fine. Got it. Please call my cell if you hear anything else." I knew she wouldn't, but I asked anyway.

"Will do." *Crunch.* "And again, our deepest sympathies."

"Why? He's not dead." I hung up the phone and swallowed the icy blizzard of rage threatening to undo me. But I had to keep my head straight. I was no good to anyone if I lost it.

I opened up my laptop and booked the first available morning flight to Mexico City. Though Justin had disappeared from the south of Mexico, just outside Palenque in the state of Chiapas, I would stop at the embassy first, gather up any details and then continue on, so I could meet with the local authorities. I could only hope my high school Spanish would get me by.

The next evening, I arrived in Mexico City, and as soon as I passed Immigration and Customs, I grabbed a cab and left a message for the cracker-eating bitch. I let her know I was staying a few blocks from the embassy off the *Paseo de la Reforma*, so I'd see her first thing in the morning. I then checked into my room, ready to pass out. It was already ten o'clock at night, and I hadn't eaten in almost a day, but that didn't stop me from hitting the mini-bar. My nerves called for something strong. Whiskey.

I kicked off my red patent leather heels, plopped down on the sofa chair, pounded down a shot, then opened my laptop. Some might think me callous and uncaring, but at a time like this, checking work email was the only thing helping me hold the line. My sanity teetered on the precipice of self-destruction and hysteria. But I refused to allow my imagination to gain a foothold, because I knew the only thing it had to offer were images of Justin screaming as his throat was slit or he was beaten with a lead pipe. The people in this country who made it a business to steal human beings for profit were no strangers to torture and violence. I remember once flipping the channels when I'd been in Buenos Aires on a business trip for a global launch of a new perfume line. (That was my specialty, high-end fragrance campaigns.) But I'd never forget the images on the evening news. Bodies lit on fire, dangling from an overpass in Mexico City. I spoke enough Spanish to understand that they'd been victims of a kidnapping, but their families either couldn't or wouldn't pay the ransom.

So yeah, maybe I was in denial or being heartless, but keeping my mind from wandering was the only thing preventing me from falling to my knees, helplessly weeping for Justin. If I were to be of any use, I had to stay strong.

That meant more whiskey.

I scooted off the bed and dug through the mini-fridge. "Shit. Really?" There was tequila, vodka, and rum, but no more whiskey. I grabbed the bottle of rum—what the hell did I care at this point?—and drank it down. "Okay. I guess I do care. Tastes like shit."

I called room service, ordered more reinforcements, spread out on the bed, and went back to my emails.

Email from my global V.P., Jim, in New York. *Please give status on Project Windpipe.* That was the code name for our holiday, celebrity singer fragrance pack. Four Grammy winners for the price of one. Plus a pair of slippers.

We will still hit the schedule. No issues, I replied.

Email from my best friend, Becca. We grew up together, and our moms were close. *Where the hell are you, Mia? Your mom says you went to see your brother? Can't believe you didn't take me. Hate you. Mean it. Call me when you get back. – Love, Becca*

I didn't want to lie to Becca, so I dropped her email in the trash file. It was better to say nothing and face her wrath later on.

Email from Sean. I gawked at his note. *Are you in NY? Hungry? I'm starved.* That was his code for "Let's hook up."

"No, I won't be in New York this week for a booty call," I mumbled aloud and took another sip of my rum. It was my own damned fault he sent me those notes. Every time I went to New York, I ended up calling him after whatever business dinner I attended. We'd usually meet at his place, tumble in the sheets, and leave it at that. We never saw each other any other time.

There was a knock at the hotel room door. "Finally." Reinforcements.

I slid off the bed and yanked open the door. "Thanks, I really—"

Two men dressed in black, wearing ski masks, pushed their way into the room. The one closest to me cupped his hand over my mouth and threw me to the floor, pinning me beneath him.

"Do not scream," he whispered with a thick Mexican accent, "or I will cut your throat."

I get that at times like this, I should've been thinking about how to survive. And maybe I was, but I quickly realized that two large, armed men against one unarmed, hundred-and-thirty-five-pound woman didn't have much of a chance of surviving. Especially given that the man standing had his gun pointed at my head.

Instead of fighting, I reverted to praying they wouldn't violate me or, worse, drag me off into the night. I couldn't help Justin if I ended up just like him.

I nodded several times, his hand smothering my whimpers of panic.

"Good." I felt his hot breath in my ear. He smelled of tequila and sweat. His free hand slithered up my torso and brutally fondled my breast. "You like that, Mia?"

Oh God. He knew my name. This wasn't some random assault.

I clenched my eyes shut and shook my head no.

"I do," he breathed into my ear. "And if you're not on a plane home by tomorrow morning, I've been given permission to take anything I want before I kill you. Nod if you understand."

I nodded and felt the sting of salty tears trickling from the corners of my eyes.

"Bien, mujer. Espero que no nos encontramos pronto."

I didn't understand, but I assumed it was one final threat.

Before I could respond, the two men were gone, the door of my hotel room shut. I rolled over on my stomach and sobbed into the palms of my hands. As soon as I was able to stand—I don't know how long it took—I was checked out and in a cab back to the airport. I figured I would be safer there until my flight.

Oh, God. Justin. What are you mixed up in?

❦

From the moment I fled that hotel room in Mexico City, I knew the situation was far worse than Justin simply being taken by *narcos* for ransom. Someone didn't want him to be found. But why? It was the only thought I'd had on the long flight back to San Francisco.

I unlocked the door to my sparsely decorated, fourth-story apartment—I traveled a lot, so what was the point of owning plants or having tons of fancy furniture no one would see or use?—and threw my bag on the living room floor. I needed sleep. I needed to clear my head.

I drew my curtains to shut out the sunlight and looked at my watch. Two ten in the afternoon. I'd only been gone one day, but it seemed like a lifetime ago.

I sank down on the couch and covered my face with my cold, cold hands. *Shit.* I had to tell someone. Especially after those bastards threatened me in the hotel room. But who could I go to? My parents? Telling them that Justin was missing would only cause them pain. And knowing my dad, stubborn man that he was, he'd be on the first plane to Mexico. I couldn't allow that. I couldn't let him get mixed up in whatever crap was going on. Involving my friends, especially Becca, wasn't an option either. She adored Justin, and it would break her heart. She also never kept anything from her mother, and her mother couldn't keep a secret if her life depended on it. My mother would be freaking out on my doorstep within the hour.

Shit. I had no idea what to do, and I needed help. *Maybe the State Department or the FBI or...*

My phone vibrated, and I slipped it from my jeans pocket. I had a message from a number in Mexico. It was over three hours old. I must've missed it while on the plane.

I held the phone to my ear. "Hello, Mia. This is Jamie Henshaw. I received your message this morning and had expected to see you today. I hope everything is all right?" It's strange how some people have the ability to say one thing but mean the opposite. "Please, call me when you get this. I have some news about your brother."

I dialed her and began pacing the floor. *Please be good news. Please be good news. Please be—*

She answered immediately.

"This is Mia Turner. I got your message."

"Mia. Ah, yes." There was some crackling in the background.

More crackers? Bitch.

"Are you still planning to come by the embassy today?" Once again, her tone sounded snide and flippant, as if she hoped I wouldn't ever darken her doorstep.

"No," I replied. "Something came up. I had to fly home this morning. I just got in."

"Oh, I see." Happy. She was happy. "I'm sorry to hear that. But I think your time would have been wasted either way. We received confirmation that your brother was not present during the incident."

"Sorry?"

"The police questioned a few locals who knew your brother. They said he'd left several days earlier."

My heart raced with joy. *Justin wasn't taken. Justin wasn't taken.*

"So where is he?"

"The authorities say he took a flight to London."

London? But Justin would have called. Or emailed. Or something. *More bullshit.*

"Are you sure? Did the police talk to his roommate?" I knew that Justin shared an apartment with some American guy, but I didn't know who he was.

"I assume so, but I don't know for sure."

Wouldn't that be an important question for her to ask the police? And now that I started to think about it, wasn't this a bit of a coincidence? I went to Mexico to find out what happened to Justin and was run out of the country. Then, all of a sudden, I'm being told he's gone somewhere else? I was being led away. Why?

"Can I have the date and flight number?" I asked.

"I'm sorry, I don't have that information. But if you want to find your brother, I suggest you start in London. And if you do track him down, please have him contact us. The local authorities want to question him. His team is still missing, and there's been no demand for a ransom."

I covered my mouth. Their poor families. "But how do I—"

The called ended abruptly.

"What in the world?" I stared at the phone, thinking that I'd just been served another helping of BS from that lady. If Justin had left Mexico, which I absolutely didn't believe, why wouldn't he have called me? And it's not like he'd just up and leave work. This archaeological dig was a big, big deal, and Justin had to answer to the foundation that funded the dig. There was no way he'd blow everything off. And if he had left, he would have checked in, and he'd know by now that something happened to his team. He'd be right back in Mexico, worried sick.

All signs pointed to something bad having happened to Justin, yet I couldn't let go of the unrealistic hope that he might be all right and that this was all some horrible misunderstanding.

I sank back down on my couch and smoothed my hands over my tangled curls. "Crap." I blew out a long breath. Okay. If Justin got on a plane, there would be a record. So who could help me find it?

The next day, after calling several airlines and being told there was no way in hell I'd be getting a hold of any flight records, I decided my best bet was the local FBI office. I'd never been inside, but had walked past it a million times. It was a 1920s-style brick building with a large marble lobby. Once past the metal detectors, I was directed to a room with a long line, where I waited for over four hours only to be told that no one could help me. If my brother was missing, I'd have to file a report with the police. When I explained he was out of the country, the man told me to file a report with the local police, then contact the nearest embassy or consulate.

"But I just need to know if he flew to the U.K.," I argued.

The agent, Agent Screwyou, who wore a shitty brown tie that matched the shitty brown frames of his thick glasses, made it clear that his patience had worn thin. "If your brother got on a plane to the U.K., then it sounds to me like he's fine. Missing, kidnapped, and dead people generally don't board planes."

Smartass. "But—"

"Go hire a private detective. We can't help you." He leaned to the side and called for the next person.

Asshole. I headed straight for the door and slipped out my phone. *Shit, Mia, what are you going to do now?*

A frigid gust tunneled between the skyscrapers through the downtown street, lashing everyone with its unwelcome chill. I walked over to a barista cart and ordered a black coffee to fit my mood and the weather. San Francisco was generally cool all year round, but when we got wind, we got *wind*. When we got rain, we got *rain*. And today, the dark gray sky threatened to unleash a fury of wetness. I instantly regretted my choice of wardrobe—a pair of red Manolo heels, a black skirt, and button-down white blouse—unfit for any severe weather. I buttoned up my camel-hair coat and sipped my hot coffee while I checked my emails on my phone. There were ten from my boss, three from Becca, and a hundred others. I'd only been out of the office three days, but the work had piled up.

Maybe I did need help. God knew I was emotionally fried, scared, and at my wits' end. So perhaps Agent Screwyou's idea wasn't so bad. I sat down at the little table beside the coffee cart and began searching for a private detective. There were hundreds, but all geared toward infidelity, background checks, or surveillance.

On the third page of searches, I found a nonprofit. The World Center for Missing Persons and Abducted Children dealt with international cases. I looked them up on the map. They were located on the other side of the city, only a fifteen-minute cab ride.

I chucked my coffee and successfully hailed a cab at the precise moment the rain started to pour. I was damned lucky; a few minutes from now, there wouldn't be a vacant cab anywhere in the city.

I slid inside and gave the address just as my phone rang. I looked at the number, but it was blocked. "Hello?" There was a ton of static on the line. "Hello?"

"Mia."

Holy shit. "Justin, is that you?"

I heard his voice again, but it was breaking up. I couldn't understand a word.

"Justin! Justin!" I repeated frantically into the phone. "Where are you?"

He spoke again, but it was pure garble.

"Justin, if you can hear me, tell me where you are!"

"Don't…come…looking. Not. Safe." The line crackled once more. "Love you. Go—" *crackle,* "bye."

The call ended. "Justin. Justin. *No.*"

Oh my god. Please call me back. Please. I stared at the phone, willing it to ring. It didn't. I dialed his cell, but it went into voicemail just as it had the last twenty times.

"Ma'am, that will be eleven dollars." Had I arrived already?

I looked up at the driver, who seemed immune to my meltdown. He probably saw his fair share of drama on a daily basis. I shoved a twenty into the slot and scrambled out of the cab.

I didn't know what to do. I was losing my mind. Justin was alive, but he needed help, and I felt so useless.

The sky shook with thunder, and the rain fell in giant sloppy drops. I slipped inside the building, dripping, sobbing, and unable to stop myself from sounding like a madwoman.

The young woman at the reception desk, a thin brunette with her hair pulled back, stood when she saw me.

I don't know why, but I held out the phone as if I believed she could magically make Justin call me again. "Please, I need help."

Her eyes widened with worry. "Of course. Come with me."

I spent the next hour telling a case manager about Justin's situation, the important parts, anyway. When I hiccupped, she gave me tea. When I cried, she gave me tissues. She was a good listener, I had to give her that, but sharing my burden out loud made it all real, and that completely unraveled me.

"Mia, you need to tell your family," she advised. Her reddish hair was pulled into a neat bun, and her brown eyes had that worn look to them, like she'd seen a lot in her lifetime, although she couldn't have been a day over fifty.

What is her name? Why can't I remember it?

"I can't tell my parents. It's too dangerous," I said.

"Okay. But you can't deal with this on your own."

"Can't you help me?" That's why I was there.

"We work with refugees from war-torn countries, looking for missing loved ones."

I opened my eyes, really opened them, and looked around the woman's cramped office with 1970s-style office furniture. Fliers for Amnesty International and crisis management informational leaflets were posted everywhere.

I sank my face into my hands. "I'm such an idiot." I'd spent the last hour pouring my heart out to this woman, and she knew I was in the wrong place. I mean, it was the right place, but not a place that could help me.

I stood and wiped away the never-ending stream of tears trickling down my raw face. "I'm so sorry. I had no idea." I dug through my purse and shoved a bunch of twenties at her. "Here. Take this. A donation."

She pushed my hand away. "No. It's all right, Mia."

"I feel terrible. I'm so embarrassed."

"Don't be. But I meant what I said; you need your family. You can't go through this alone."

I nodded and headed for the front door. It was pitch-black outside, and the rain hadn't let up one bit, not that I cared. "Thank you. I-I—never mind. Just…thank you."

My red heels hit one giant puddle after another as I slogged down the street. *What was her name? Why can't I remember it? I'm losing my mind, that's why. I'm a mess. A mess. And Justin needs me. You'd think I'd have the decency to remember that woman's name after she sat there for an hour listening to me—*

"Mia!"

The scream broke me from my jumbled stream of thoughts. I turned my head and saw the young receptionist chasing after me down the sidewalk.

"Here. Take this." She shoved a piece of paper into my hand. A bolt of thunder licked the sky, and the woman jumped. "It's an address. But you didn't get it from me. Okay?"

"For what?" I asked.

"Not what. *Who.*" She flashed a nervous glance over her shoulder. "He might be able to help you."

"Who is he?" I asked. But honestly, I didn't care. Help was help.

"My sister's husband was kidnapped during a trip to Colombia. This man found him. They say he can find anything or anyone." She paused. "For a price. A steep price. But promise you won't tell him who sent you. He doesn't like people talking."

I didn't understand why. If this man made it his business to find people, then wouldn't he want a referral?

"Just..." Once again, she glanced over her shoulder toward her building. Why did I feel like we were dealing drugs or guns or something? "Just ask him his price. Tell him that everything has a price, and you want to know his."

"Uhhh, thanks." Just what I needed, some asshole extortionist to suck my bank account dry.

Perhaps sensing my apprehension, she looked me in the eyes. And like an old Frankenstein movie, the lightning struck, allowing me to see her concerned face. "He can help you, Mia. I swear it. But the man is...he's..." She stopped herself. "I gotta go." She headed back toward the building.

"What's his name?" I called out.

She stopped just short of the building's entrance. "King. His name is King."

CHAPTER THREE

As I stumbled my way through the rain, my imagination insisted on punishing me with horrible visions of Justin calling out from some dark, damp hole in the ground, starving to death, his body battered and bruised.

You don't know that, Mia.

Still, I didn't dare hope that Justin was somewhere safe, simply hiding out. When he'd called me while I was in the cab, his voice on the phone had sounded forlorn and desperate, not the voice of a man lying low on a tropical island or somewhere in the U.K. under an alias.

No, I knew my brother better than anyone. Even in high school when most brothers and sisters avoided each other, especially if one was a super geek—Justin—and the other had a pretty fabulous social life—me—we always hung out. I had Justin's back, and he had mine. When we both went away to college, him to Stanford, and me to the University of Pennsylvania on a partial scholarship, we still managed to talk or email at least once a week. Justin was more than a brother; he was my best friend, even closer than Becca.

My phone vibrated in my pocket, and I quickly dug it out. *Shit.* It was my mother. I couldn't face her. I couldn't tell her about Justin. She'd be devastated. I'd simply have to let her continue thinking I was still in Mexico visiting Justin.

I slid the phone back inside my cold, damp coat and palmed the crinkled slip of paper the young receptionist had given me. I stopped in another doorway and used my phone to illuminate the writing. The guy's office was back downtown, near the Financial District and about a ten-minute walk from my apartment. I looked at my watch. It was almost seven o'clock, but perhaps someone might be working late.

I came up onto the main avenue, and as if an angel were watching out for me, an empty cab stopped. Grateful for the heat and dryness, I jumped in and used the short ride to rehearse my words. Whoever this King guy was, he'd want to discuss "his price," as the receptionist said. I had some money set aside, but not much. My student loans still sucked up a hefty portion of my income. I figured I could sell off some things—what little bit of furniture I owned and a few pieces of jewelry— but without involving my parents, it wouldn't amount to much. That meant I'd have to negotiate.

The cab pulled up to the mouth of a dark, dead-end street that had been permanently barricaded with cement posts. It looked like one of those alleyways used for touristy outdoor cafés and restaurants during the day.

I paid the driver and found the address near the very end. There was a small lobby with nothing in it other than a directory and a stainless steel elevator. The woman hadn't told me which suite, but two businesses occupied every floor except for the sixth, which only had the letter "K" written in the directory.

I got inside the elevator, shivering to the bone, and stared at my shabby reflection in the gleaming stainless steel door. I was a mess. My blonde waves dripped like wet spaghetti, and my camel-hair coat was in no better shape.

"Great." I grabbed a rubber band from my purse and quickly wound my hair into a little knot at the nape of my neck. I shrugged off my coat and tucked my blouse back into my black skirt.

When the elevator doors slid open, I stepped out into another small lobby, completely empty, with only one door. I eyeballed the gold-plated plaque beside it with the letter "K" in a big bold font. This had to be it.

I tried the handle, relieved to find the door unlocked. "Hello?" I poked my head inside the empty loft with exposed pipes along the painted, white ceiling. The only light came from a lonely lamp atop an antique desk at the far end, just a few feet from another door. "Hello?"

I stepped all the way inside and instantly felt an arctic-like chill sweep through the room. *Fuck. Why did I come here?* The vibe was far more depressing than the space inside my head.

Suddenly, the room filled with a delicious scent. Spice with citrus and something else.

"You're late," said a menacingly deep voice.

"Crap!" I swiveled in my squishy red heels toward the shadow of a man lurking in the obscured corner. I couldn't see much, but he was tall, his frame lean, but not thin. His muscular silhouette immediately put me on edge.

He stepped into the faint sphere of light radiating from the desk lamp, allowing me to get a look at some of him. He wore a nicely tailored black suit, crisp white shirt, and dark silk tie—navy blue?—however, those little details were not what my brain chose to hone in on.

His lips were full and sinfully sexy, framed by a thick, well-manicured patch of coalmine black whiskers.

"Are you K-K-King?"

"You're dripping on my fucking floor. Don't you own an umbrella?"

Something about the way he spoke, that heavy voice, the way it carried a certain authority, had an instant effect; it scared the shit out of me.

"Put your coat on the chair," he demanded.

"But I—"

"We both know why you're here. So just do it."

Had the receptionist who'd given me his number called him? Hadn't she said she didn't want him to know she'd sent me?

"Is something the matter with your hearing?" His rich, syrupy male voice hadn't risen above a shallow whisper, but the tone was more powerful than any threat.

I glanced over at the lonely desk. The only chair in the room was behind it. I walked over, thinking that this had been a mistake in a long line of mistakes I'd made that day. Still, there wasn't anything I wouldn't do to save Justin, including giving my life.

I laid my coat over the back of the chair and set my purse down atop the desk. I glanced back over toward the corner—

His hot breath bathed the back of my neck, and the heat of his body pressed against me, paralyzing every muscle in my body. *Oh shit.*

"You're not my usual type," his low voice crawled into my ears, "but I think I'll make do." His hot hands brushed a few loose strands of my wet hair to one side, leaving behind an icy trail of tingles.

My mind quickly went into self-preservation mode. *Weapon, Mia. Find a weapon.* Lamp. Phone. I had a sharp heel on my shoe, I could—

He placed a slow kiss on that little spot just behind my ear. I wanted to scream; however, my instincts told me to keep calm. And when his tongue began massaging that spot, it didn't matter what my brain said; it was as if he held some power over me.

"Mmm…" he said. "I bet you taste sweet."

Mia, you have to fight him off. A quick blow to his ribs with my elbow or a thrust with my heel to his groin. Either would buy me time to make it to the stairs.

Shit. Where are the stairs?

His hand slipped around and cupped my breast through my damp shirt, which triggered me to make my move, but he blocked my elbow and somehow caught my wrist. I felt my bones bending from the pressure of his grip. Then, with a swiftness my mind couldn't process, he twisted my arm behind my back and pushed me face down onto the desk.

"What are you doing?" I cried.

"What does it look like?" He pushed on my arm, and the sharp, unbearable pain of my shoulder pulling from its socket made me moan in agony.

He chuckled softly, and I felt the hardness of his stiff cock pressing into my ass. His free hand slid under my skirt, between my thighs, and cupped me from behind. His hot fingers forcefully stroked me through my panties. "How did you know I wanted to play rough tonight?"

"Please," I begged. "I'll do anything for Justin. But not this."

His hand froze. "Justin?" he snarled. "Who the fuck is Justin?"

"My little brother."

"Who sent you?" he growled.

"I—I heard about you through a friend."

Without relinquishing his grip on my arm, he removed his hand from between my legs. He decided that grinding my head into the desk was a better option. "Who. Sent. You?"

"I'm not going to tell you," I mumbled, half my face plastered against the polished, antique wood that smelled of stale cigars and varnish. "Do you want to talk price or not?"

He laughed, a sinister, cruel laugh, and released me. I quickly spun, ready to beat the man with my fists, but he caught my arm again, and when I looked into his eyes, I knew I'd never forget them. Not in my dreams, not in the daylight, not on my deathbed. They were a light shimmery gray, fringed with black lashes, and filled with something ominous. I suddenly didn't see a dangerous, and perhaps violent, thirty-year-old man with a flawlessly masculine face standing before me in an expensive suit. I saw a man with deep trenches of scars on his soul from a lifetime of greed and unhappiness. Whatever had happened to him, whatever had gone wrong in his life, it must've been bad.

I continued to stare, now seeing a storm of raw pain, loneliness, and anger raging behind those eyes. An unwelcome wave of sympathy washed over me. What had happened to him?

The man's cold gaze wandered down to my lips as if committing every crease to memory. "What's your name?"

"M-M-Mia? Mia Turner?" Why had I made it sound like a damned question?

There was a faint knock at the door, and we both turned our heads. In walked a woman, legs as long as my entire body, wearing a short black trench coat. Her brown hair was swept up into knot, and her lips were blood red. She regarded King, then looked at me. "Am I interrupting?"

"No. Miss Turner was just leaving," said King.

"That's it?" No apology? No inquiry as to why I was even there?

"Not unless you plan on laying yourself back over this desk, Miss Turner." He shamelessly glanced down at his obvious erection.

My jaw dropped.

"I thought not." He shrugged, and then his eyes flashed to the door. "Good night."

"Asshole," I hissed under my breath.

His bitter gaze dropped to my face, and he smiled, two deep grooves appearing in each cheek. If that smile had been my first glimpse ever of this man, I would have melted from its charm. But now I knew that any civility or good manners were a shallow façade.

"That was uncalled for. You came here and flaunted your wet little self. How was I supposed to know?" He looked amused.

I grabbed my coat and purse and stepped around the desk. I suddenly wanted to cry. My nerves were far beyond sizzled, and my ability to think rationally had abandoned me long, long ago. Yet, when I reached the door, I couldn't leave. I'd come there for a reason. A damned important one.

I turned and looked at him. "I was told you can find anything or anyone. Is that true?"

His brows flinched with wicked joy. "For a price. A price I already know you're unwilling to pay."

Sex. The asshole had been serious? He wanted sex?

I looked down at my soggy, red heels. Could I do that for Justin? Barter with my flesh and bones to save him? How far would Justin go for me if the roles were reversed? He wouldn't likely object to someone demanding sex; however, he would put his life on the line for me. In fact, he had. When we were in high school, he'd saved me from a couple of drunken shitheads at a party. I was young and stupid and had too much to drink myself. Luckily, Justin had been there, but it had landed him in the hospital. He'd been beaten within an inch of his life, and I'd never forgiven myself. Not even to this day.

But Justin was always there to look after me. Always. So, yes, I'd do anything for him. My only question was, could this man, King, truly help me?

I lifted my chin and stared King down, resisting the urge to topple over and faint. "Fine. If you save Justin, I'll-I'll…" I swallowed. "Do *that*. If that's what you want." I couldn't say the word sex or anything close to it.

King laughed. The beautiful, elegant woman, who'd been standing there the entire time, also looked entertained as hell.

"I have her for sex," King glanced at the woman, "and I'm sure for the six hundred I'm paying, she'll satisfy all my needs. You, on the other hand…" He paused, and one side of his mouth turned up. "You look like you'd break."

The way he'd said "break" made it sound like he'd enjoy doing it.

Just when I thought I couldn't feel any more helpless and weak, this bastard proved me wrong. I wanted to crawl inside a hole and die. How had I gotten to this place in my life? One week ago, I'd been a strong, independent woman with her whole life ahead of her. The perfect job. Happy. In control. Now...

Crap. What was wrong with me? Maybe King was right; I would break. It took less than a handful of days for life to show me how fragile I was. Yet I couldn't help but pretend I still maintained some semblance of self-respect. Even if it was a lie.

"Did you see me crumble a few moments ago when you tried to screw me over your desk?" I reached for the door handle. "So don't flatter yourself."

"My price is you."

I stilled halfway out the door and gazed back into those predatory, hypnotic, gray eyes. He terrified me. "I don't understand."

"I'll find your brother, and in exchange, I own you."

"Own me?"

"Those are my terms." He crossed his arms over his chest, his thick biceps stretching the black fabric of his expensive blazer. "You want me to find someone dear to you, Miss Turner. Then I ask for something dear in return. Your obedient servitude. Indefinitely."

What a sadistic bastard. He'd already stolen my last soggy crumb of dignity.

"To do what?" I asked.

He laughed, causing deep creases to form on both sides of his gorgeous, wicked mouth. "As you are told, Miss Turner. As you are told."

"I'm in advertising. What use would I be to you?"

The scowl on his perfect, handsome face chilled my blood. It said, *Don't ever question me again.* But his lips said something different: "Yes or no, Miss Turner. Yes or no?"

He couldn't be serious. This had to be some sadistic game of chicken. Because clearly he was the sort of man who enjoyed controlling people, breaking them down. Yes, we'd already established that. So perhaps he didn't think I had the balls to accept his terms. But I did. I'd do anything for Justin. Anything.

"Okay. Fine."

King dipped his head as if he were a gracious gentleman accepting a duel. "Very good. Now, if you'll excuse us; please shut the door behind you," he commanded. "And Mia?"

"Yes." I glanced over my shoulder one last time.

"Be here. Monday. Six a.m. sharp. And don't be late, or the deal is off."

❧

Hyperventilating, I made my way outside, where the rain greeted me once more. *What have you done, Mia? Something isn't right with that man,* I told myself, trying to wipe away my tears with my sopping wet coat. *Lord, I can't breathe. I can't breathe.* I stumbled and nearly fell, at which point I decided to take a moment in a nearby doorway to catch my breath. Meanwhile, my mind raced in sickening loops to make sense of everything that had just happened. "I own you," he'd said. What did he really mean by that? What sort of person even said that?

Suddenly, I caught a whiff of that addictive smell from King's office. I leaned forward a bit to see who was on the sidewalk.

Oh my Lord. It was King. Alone. Had he sent his company home?

Or maybe the jackass is really a jack rabbit.

Not likely. Men like that would never compromise their egos by being a two-second wonder.

So what made him change his mind and forgo his "date"?

In any case, I decided to follow him. I needed to know who I'd bartered away my life to—if that's what had really just happened. Was he the devil? A psychopath?

Doing my best to stay hidden in the shadows, I followed King as he walked toward the heart of the Financial District, not too far from the renovated loft he called his office. When he turned off the busy downtown street and disappeared inside a building just down another alley, I had to see what it was. A strip club, perhaps? A sports bar for arrogant, sadistic bastards? I froze and stared at the solid black doors. No signage. No numbers. Just a plain red welcome mat to match the red bulb dangling overhead. I reached for the handles and stopped. What if he was inside? What if he saw me? He'd know I'd been following him, and he didn't seem like the sort of man who would appreciate it. But I needed to know something, anything, about this man who scared the hell out of me and who I'd promised to practically enslave myself to only moments earlier, simply based on a hope that he might find Justin.

What was I thinking? So stupid. The man is completely insane. I wasn't going back there, I decided now that my head felt clearer.

"It's members only, Miss Turner," King's voice projected from behind me. "And I sincerely doubt you'll find what you're looking for inside. Justin was last seen in Palenque, was he not?"

"But how-how-how…" I could do little more than stutter like a fool. I'd just seen King go inside seconds earlier. Had he known I was following him and come back out through a side door? And how did he know where Justin had disappeared from? "You—but—how…?"

King's straight black brows bowed into beautiful little arches as he laughed. It was the second time I'd seen those deep smile lines, and they were just as captivating as the first. And if I were only some random woman walking by, I would probably trip. The way he stood there, arms crossed, his broad, square shoulders draped in fine fabric, he could be mistaken for a real man. A perfect, stunningly good-looking man.

But I wasn't random. And he terrified me. So I ran like a coward, his deep laughter mocking me until I was out of earshot.

Once home, I spent half the night trying to talk myself out of ever going back to see King, but I couldn't help wondering how he'd known about Justin's location. Perhaps I'd said something? No, I hadn't. I'd gone over that bizarre and disturbing scene at his office a hundred times. So how had he known? Was he really able to "find anyone or anything?" And if I returned, what would happen to me? *"I own you"*? He couldn't have meant that literally. Could he?

Thankfully, he'd made it clear that it wasn't about sex. So exactly what was the deal? What would I be doing for him if I went back? Scrub his toilets? Arrange hookers to come to his office? His words, "As you are told," left a lot of latitude.

Don't be a coward, Mia. You have to go back. Because if this man was truly able to help, I owed it to Justin. *Okay, I'll go Monday morning, like he said. But only to ask questions.*

He would have to explain how he would find Justin. If he was really a missing persons badass, then he'd have to convince me. And first thing tomorrow morning, I would go right back to that building King had gone into and find out what it was.

CHAPTER FOUR

After the longest week of my life, avoiding my parents (who thought I was still in Mexico) and trying not to crush under the weight of my worry, I showed up Monday morning, on time just as King asked.

The office was empty. A note stuck to the lamp simply said:

Sit. Wait.
– K

I scratched my head. He wanted me to wait? But hadn't he demanded punctuality?

I knocked on the locked door, which I assumed led to his personal office, but there was no reply.

Great. I didn't know which was worse, being in the presence of the man who scared the ever-living hell out of me or being alone in his big empty loft-slash-office. Even during the day, the place had a very, very unsettling vibe. The white walls were bare. The floors were dark. The air was cold.

I began to hum "She Loves You" by the Beatles, something I did whenever I felt nervous. After about ten minutes of standing around in my heels— a pair of black Jimmy's with very sharp points that could easily double as daggers—I reluctantly decided to sit at the lonely desk. I hadn't forgotten how he'd used it against me, but tried not to think about it. Instead, I ended up chewing on how little I knew about this man, King. I knew he had an empty office, he liked expensive suits, he smelled incredible, and was the biggest bastard I'd ever met. Oh, and he also belonged to a really weird club. 10 Club.

Yes, I had returned to those mysterious doors the morning following my unsavory introduction to King. Inside were an empty hallway and a lone elevator with a golden plaque to the side: *10 Club. Members Only.* Later, when I got home, I looked it up. The club was for people of "considerable social standing" worth ten or more. Billion, that was. I'd thought it sounded pretentious—perfect for a man like King—but what struck me as odd was the lack of any further information. One would think such a club might have some philanthropy kudos, really nice ads, or fancy pamphlets. Something. But the club was just as mysterious as King. Who, by the way, didn't even show up in a Google search ("king detective," "king agency," "king 10 club"). Nothing. The man had to be living under an alias.

After thirty minutes of waiting, my humming ceased working its magic, so I got out my phone and answered emails as a distraction. One hour later, still no sign of King. There were no signs of any clients, either. No one came in. The phone didn't ring. The place felt like a ghost town.

"Just missing the tumbleweed," I mumbled. And that's when I got to thinking. He probably worked out of some other office. Maybe he had a day job— sadistic investment banker?—and kept this office for his side business or hooker rendezvous. And he probably had no intention of showing up early. Perhaps he would make me wait the entire day just to prove a point.

Fine. If that's what it took, I could wait. In fact, I'd go out at noon for lunch, grab my laptop and come back here to get some work done. Which is what I did. I didn't see the point of being bored or unproductive. Not when I had five hundred emails to answer, including four from Sean asking why I hadn't come to New York lately and why I hadn't answered any of his emails. I responded by saying that I was sorry, but I'd been tied up on a special project. He'd probably think I was finally seeing someone seriously.

I managed to get through another one hundred emails of extreme distress from my team at work. The holiday fragrance campaign was going to hell because of an unforeseen supply issue with the packager. Great. Now the rest of my life was falling apart. And King was nowhere to be found. I needed to talk to him about his real "price" because I couldn't just sit around here all day. And while thinking it over this last week, no way had he been serious that he wanted to "own me." How ridiculous. But as five o'clock rolled around, I began to wonder if he'd ever show. I'd give him another hour; then I was out of there.

A minute before six, I shut down my computer and slid it into my case. When I looked up, King's masculine figure filled the doorway. I hadn't even heard the door open or close.

I stood up and stared at the man. He stared back. I was about to say something such as, "Nice of you to show up," but then he walked right past me as if I wasn't even there. He entered his office and closed the door.

What in the world?

"I can't do this," I muttered. There was no way he was going to be of any help finding Justin. That woman who'd referred him had to be off her rocker or getting some kind of kickback. Yes, maybe this was a scam targeted at desperate people with missing loved ones.

Of course! I bet they wandered into that center for missing persons all the time. It would explain why the woman had been so nervous, how King had known about Palenque, and why he acted like a depraved sleazeball. Because he was.

I'm such an idiot. I grabbed my stuff to leave, but then the phone on the desk rang. At first, I wasn't going to pick it up; however, something urged me to do it. "He-hello?"

"When your brother called you the other day, did you believe him?" It was King's deep, unforgettable voice.

"Sorry?" Was the guy really calling me from the other room? I couldn't decide if that was eccentric or just rude and creepy.

"It's a simple question, Miss Turner. Did you believe him? Did you believe that he didn't want you to come looking for him?"

How did King know that? I hadn't told anyone the details of our conversation, not even the lady at the Center for Missing Persons.

"I don't—ummm…I don't know," I replied, shocked as hell.

"And did you believe Jamie Henshaw when she said your brother got on a plane to London?"

"How do you know about that?" I asked.

"It's a simple question, Miss Turner. Yes or no?"

"No."

"That will be all. Good night. Oh—and, Miss Turner, you work for me now. You will call your office and resign your other job immediately. You can also tell your lover you won't be seeing him anymore. You'll have no time for trips to New York."

What? He knew about Sean, too? And he couldn't possibly be serious about me quitting.

"So you want to hire me? To do what?" I asked.

"Hiring implies I will pay you. However, may I remind you that you are the one who is paying me. With your life."

He was serious? "How do you expect me to live?"

He laughed. "You no longer have a life. You are mine—a term you've already agreed to. Just as I have agreed to find your brother, which I will. As for the 'what' you will do? The answer is simple: as you are told, Miss Turner. Anything I ask."

"But I—"

"I am not the sort of man who deals kindly with welshers, Miss Turner. Are you a welsher?"

"No."

"Good. Because I would hate for you to find out what I do to people who displease me."

What the f…?

"Have a good evening." He hung up, and my jaw dropped.

I barely pulled myself back from charging to his door and pounding it down.

Instead, I left. I needed to get out of there, to breathe. All of my assumptions about King were wrong. He wasn't just an eccentric, wealthy bastard. He was the devil. Downright evil. And how had he known the details about the call from my brother or the embassy?

Whoever King was, he was well connected.

And dangerous.

Yes. And now you're his assistant?

෩∙෬

Proving once more that I'd misjudged King and the seedy depths of his malevolence, I spent the next three weeks sitting alone in that cold, creepy office, watching the clock tick away on my brother's life. Each evening at six o'clock, King would show up, go into his office, and then call to dismiss me. A twisted and bizarre little ritual. And each evening I promised myself I would confront him, only to find myself paralyzed. The ominous man's presence did something to me that I couldn't begin to articulate. It was a sickly sensation combined with a powerful urge to gawk. On the exterior, he was unsettlingly beautiful, and on the inside, he was wicked. But nevertheless, he was still just a man. So why did I fall apart in his presence?

If I weren't so desperate and so absolutely convinced that this man, King, could do what he said—hunt down Justin or punish me if I "displeased him"—I wouldn't have kept coming back. But I had, occupying myself by making inquiries with officials in Mexico. Zero luck. I had even made a list and called every person who'd ever been in contact with Justin, but it was like he'd disappeared off the face of the planet.

So why hadn't King started looking? At least, that's what I assumed. He hadn't given me reason to believe otherwise. Instead, he made me sit in that office. Why? Did he want to see how far he could push me?

Of course. The man was not only cruel, he was sadistic. A statement I felt with severe conviction when days earlier, I secretly moved my belongings into storage and set up camp in a cheap motel. And knowing without a paying job I couldn't afford even that, I stooped to calling Becca with some BS story about how just as soon as I was back in S.F. from my fake trip in a few days, I'd need to crash at her place for a while due to a nonexistent mold problem.

With everything else going on, lying to her was a new low point in my life, only surpassed by the moment when I called my boss to resign from my dream job.

I kept telling myself, over and over again, that I had to do this for Justin. That his life was more valuable than any job or apartment, but that didn't mean losing them felt good.

Then, just when I'd been pushed that last inch, ready to unleash a fury, King called. "It is time, Miss Turner," he'd said.

"King?"

"No. It's your fucking fairy godmother, Miss Turner. And your wish has been granted."

I had been speechless. He gave no explanation as to why it was time. He gave no destination details until I got to the airport, passport in hand.

And now, as I stood in line after a five-hour flight, waiting to pass Immigration at the Mexico City airport and head to my connecting flight, I fended off those dark thoughts telling me that this trip would be the death of me. I should never have lied to my mother and father, who believed I was still in Mexico and due home at any moment. Yes, they had actually believed the story I fed them about Justin and I having some major vacay time coming and that we would be in Cancun before visiting all of the Yucatan ruins. "No cell phone access for a few weeks," I'd said. Such a stupid lie. Cell phones were just about everywhere in the world these days. And who took vacations longer than a week or two? Not many. But they'd bought it, allowing me to hide the truth. For a while, anyway.

"Mia Turner?"

Bag slung over my shoulder, passport in hand, I lifted my troubled gaze from the floor. A cold stare from a Mexican official in a dark green uniform greeted me. Two soldiers with rifles stood behind him. All three men were about my height—five-six—but what they lacked in stature, they made up for in deadly weapons.

My stomach fell into a tailspin. "Yes?"

The room of queued-up passengers turned to stare. Anyone within twenty feet stepped away.

"Come with us, please," said the official.

"Is something wrong?" I asked. My heart thumped wildly inside my chest.

"We warned you not to return," he whispered.

Shit.

⁂

Those terrifying men that night in the hotel room four weeks earlier had left no doubt in my mind that they'd meant what they'd said. They would kill me if I returned looking for Justin. But I'd mistakenly believed the incident was connected to a well-organized group of lowlife narcos who'd taken my brother. I thought, perhaps, they'd been watching me. Maybe watching my entire family, trying to figure out how much we were worth before they issued a ransom. But now, this second time through, I knew differently. I had been detained before officially entering the country.

What the hell was Justin involved with? And why the hell hadn't I told King about my prior trip to Mexico City? I suppose I never had the chance, but not telling him felt like a mistake. A big, big mistake.

One of the soldiers handcuffed me in front of the onlookers from my flight. The three men then walked me down a long, narrow passage and led me inside a small room with dirty, blue walls. No mirrors, no table or chairs, just a room with a door. The soles of my brown suede boots stuck to the grimy floor. I hoped it wasn't dried blood.

"Why am I here?" I tugged at the hem of my white turtleneck, not knowing what else to say, but the men kept to their task of stripping me of my watch, cell phone, and other personal belongings, including my passport. Then they left without a word.

"Crap." I paced the length of the room for several hours. No bathroom, no water, no answers as to what would happen next. My imagination had a field day.

When the door finally swung open, I stilled. The man wore a cheap, gray suit and even cheaper cologne. His deep pockmarks and greasy smile screamed criminal. I placed my back to the wall furthest from the door.

"*Señorita* Turner," he said. *Why is his voice familiar?* "I am Inspector Guzman of the *Agencia Federal de Investigaciones*."

I remained as still as my weak knees allowed.

He glanced at someone in the hallway and flicked his fingers. In walked a soldier with a chair. He placed it down directly in front of me, and Agent Guzman sat with his legs wide open.

Nice view. Thanks.

He smiled and flashed a set of gold-capped teeth. "Do you know why you are here?" he asked with a thick accent.

"No." I shoved my hand into my jeans pocket, wishing my cell phone was there so I could call for help.

He slipped a cigarette from his pocket and lit it. He sucked hard, savoring the long puff, and blew it toward the ceiling.

He was enjoying this.

He took another long puff and blew it out. "Your brother is a smuggler. We believe that someone very close to him, someone living on the other side of the border, was assisting him."

"What?" I straightened my spine. "That's bullshit. Justin was a scientist. He detests drugs."

Agent Guzman flicked his ashes on the floor. "I did not say drugs, Miss Turner. I said smuggler. Of artifacts."

Justin was smuggling? First of all, I didn't believe it. Second, nothing he dug up was of any interest to anyone except other geeky archaeologists or a museum. Third, Justin was never in it for the money. He loved the hunt. He loved learning. But it didn't matter what I thought.

"You think I was helping him?" I asked.

Agent Guzman stood and closed the gap between us, placing both arms on either side of my head. He blew his disgusting, sour breath mixed with cigarette smoke in my face.

"Mr. Vaughn," he whispered in my ear, "wants his things returned."

Mr. Vaughn. I had no idea who that was.

"Until this happens," Guzman continued, "you are to remain in our custody."

"I don't know anything. I just want to find my brother."

"I find that hard to believe, Mia. We saw Justin's phone records. You are the only one he called on a frequent basis." He snapped his fingers, and in walked that same soldier armed with a rifle. "I suggest you cooperate..." he dipped his head, "fully."

The soldier smiled with a sinister grin and shut the door. He propped his rifle in the corner and then undid the top button of his pants.

I glanced back at the agent, who reminded me of a hungry lion about to enjoy watching a helpless animal get torn to shreds.

"Whoa." I held out my hands. "I'm sure that this is a mistake—"

"There is no *pinche* mistake," Guzman hissed. "But we will enjoy your company all the same."

There was a knock at the door. The sliver of a petite woman's face showed through the crack. She wore a dark green military uniform. I couldn't understand what they said, but the agent and soldier cursed before promptly leaving the room without giving me a second thought, leaving the door partially open.

I leaned over and tried not to vomit. *Holy fuck. Holy fuck. This can't be happening.*

When the door swung open, King's imposing frame and tailored black suit were the last things I expected to see.

He leaned against the door jamb and crossed his arms. His light-gray eyes slowly washed over my body, his unsettling expression somewhere between hunger and irritation and, well, relief. "Detained, Miss Turner? Aren't you full of surprises?"

CHAPTER FIVE

Bewildered, I gazed at the unearthly perfection of King's masculine face—the line of his angular jaw, the sharp planes of his cheekbones, the fullness of his lips—as he scowled from the doorway of the airport interrogation room.

"You and I need to have a little talk, Miss Turner."

I couldn't agree more, but given what had just happened and that I was now in the imposing presence of an emotionally charged King, I lacked the ability to form a coherent word.

"What's the matter, Miss Turner? *Federale* got your tongue?"

"N-no. Not exactly." However, had King arrived a few minutes later, I was certain the *federale* or his army boy would have had another part of me. *Sick bastards.*

"How did you know I was here?" I asked.

He sneered. "I generally know everything worth knowing. Except when people, foolish girls in particular, decide to hide things from me. In that case, bad things happen. But not to me. You remember that next time, Miss Turner." He gestured for me to leave the room, but my feet had stuck to the floor, both literally and figuratively. "You are welcome to stay, but I have an appointment I cannot miss." He glanced at his watch, and I caught a glimpse of a few thick black lines on his forearm. A tattoo. I found it hard to believe such an uptight man, so preoccupied with his immaculate appearance, would waste his time with body art.

"Are they really going to let me walk out of here?" I asked.

"Yes."

Okay. I wanted to ask how—had he paid them off?—but it seemed much more important to get the hell out of there.

I slid past him and ignored the sensual chills that swept through my body when my arm grazed his chest. I ignored his menacing presence behind me as the overhead lights flickered along the lonely hallway.

"Take a right," he said. "Up the stairs."

Were we in the basement? I didn't remember going down any stairs.

I walked up a flight and exited through a set of heavy steel doors that led outside. I paused to figure out where I was. It was nighttime now, and the roar of airplane engines filled my ears.

I glanced back at King. Even now, standing on a windy, noisy landing strip, having rescued me from whatever-the-fuck that had been back there, he looked so calm, like an elegant gentleman on his way to a power-meeting to talk numbers and sip cognac. Did anything rattle his cage? Anything at all?

"This way." He jerked his head toward a private jet parked alongside a small hangar. I followed him across the asphalt, up the Jetway stairs, and boarded, shocked as hell when I saw my belongings neatly deposited in the first row of black leather seats.

"How did you get my stuff back?"

King ignored my question. "Why didn't you tell me that you'd been run out of Mexico City four weeks ago?" he snapped.

"You didn't ask."

A frigid glaze washed over his gorgeous, supremely masculine face. "I shouldn't have to. And let's get one thing clear, Miss Turner, if you keep something from me again, your brother won't be the only person missing. That's not a threat, by the way, but a warning. I can't help you if I don't know everything."

I glanced down at my feet, holding back that something horrible building inside my chest. "There's not much to tell. They were wearing masks. They broke into my hotel room and told me to go home, to stop asking questions." That's when it hit me. That agent's voice had sounded familiar. "I think it was that Guzman guy."

King dipped his head and drilled me with his pale gray eyes which said, *No shit, woman.* Instead, his mouth said, "Did they touch you?" His gazed quickly flashed to my breasts. It made me feel vulnerable and naked, like he could see right through my snug white turtleneck.

I crossed my arms over my chest and looked away. "No. Not really. They just threatened to."

King hiked up his sleeve and looked at his watch again. My eyes gravitated toward that tattoo, but he was too quick to let me see it. "Anything else I should know?"

He already knew about Justin's phone call and the calls from the embassy. Aside from that, there wasn't much to tell. "No."

"Very well." He dipped his head. "Have a pleasant evening."

Pleasant? That's all he had to say? King and I had made a deal. He would find Justin, and I would work for him. Indefinitely. It was a deal that I didn't fully understand or know what would happen if I didn't keep it, other than something bad, but I'd made it anyway, dammit, and it had cost me my job and apartment. I'd given up everything just in the hopes that King could help me find my brother. Instead, I'd lost three entire weeks of precious time! Waiting! I'd been left to stew inside my head, playing Pong with my imagination. *Justin's not dead. Yes, he is. Just wait, King will help you. No, he won't. If you push, King won't lift a finger. But if I do nothing, Justin will die.*

"Goddammit, King!" I screamed, no longer able to contain the toxic emotions. "What the hell is going on? Who were those people? How did you find me?"

The clean air inside the cabin seemed to vaporize into a sour, poisonous gas. I could barely breathe.

"Answering your questions, Miss Turner, isn't part of our deal," he growled.

He turned away, and I grabbed his arm. It was as hard as a block of cement.

He effortlessly slid from my grip and glared down at me. Though he was about six-three, which made him seven or eight inches taller, he felt like a menacing giant five stories tall.

Still, I didn't care. "I'm changing our deal!" I screamed.

"You think you can?" he responded calmly. "You think you're in a position to challenge me? I *own* you, Mia. I control what happens to you. I can arrange to have you thrown right back in that interrogation room."

He had spoken to me as if I were his dog. No. Even lower than that. He'd spoken to me as if I would be the luckiest person in the world if he bothered to let me lick his perfectly polished, black shoes. And it seriously set me off. I wasn't worthless. I wasn't his...his...

"Fuck you, King. I'm not one of those whores you bring to your office. I'm not going to bend over and take it from you."

He laughed coolly into the air. His broad shoulders shook beneath his fine black suit.

"What's so funny?" I fumed.

"You. You're funny. I just saved you, and you accuse me of treating you poorly." His deep smile lines faded back into his cheeks as he smoothed his hand over his raven black hair, not that anything was out of place. Everything about the man, on his exterior anyway, was spotless perfection, right down to the evenly groomed growth of black stubble on his perfect jaw.

His hard gaze landed on my tearing eyes, then drifted down to my chest again. "Besides, if you were my whore," he said with the crisp pronunciation of a well-bred gentleman, "right now you'd be sucking my cock, not telling me to fuck myself."

He turned away, clearly knowing his sharp words had shocked the fight right out of me. "I'll see you at Palenque."

"Where are you going?" I blurted, knowing he wouldn't answer and wondering why I cared.

To my utter shock, he stilled and looked over his shoulder at me. I noticed the muscles of his square jaw ticking. "I have some unfinished business with Agent Guzman. I take offence when people touch what's mine." He disappeared down the stairs.

Touch what's his? Did he mean me? Was he going to do something to that Guzman guy?

"You should be careful," said a strange male voice.

I jumped in my skin.

A man with short, messy, blonde hair, in his mid-thirties, wearing a short-sleeved pilot's shirt and black slacks, hovered in the doorway of the cockpit. His thick, heavily tattooed arms—banners with names and dates—were on full display as he gripped the frame of the doorway overhead.

"Sorry?" I said.

He flashed a boyish grin. "Questions piss King off almost as much as when people fuck with his stuff."

"Who are you?" I asked.

The man looked at his watch. "It's time to go." He smiled again. "I'm Mack. And you'd better buckle your seatbelt; it's going to get bumpy."

Going to?

෨⊷ঔ

Shortly after takeoff, the pilot, who flew alone, made a quick visit to the cabin and checked on me. That meant ensuring me he'd switched over to autopilot—yeah, I may have freaked out a little— before pointing me to the snacks, blankets, and safety equipment. It felt surreal flying in a fully loaded private plane—six rows of reclining black leather seats, a large flat-screen TV, and full bar.

Of course, I immediately went for reinforcements: whiskey. I drank two shots and poured a triple. My head hurt, my heart hurt, and my body ached from overexposure to violence-provoked adrenaline. However, closing my eyes was the last thing I wanted; I might see images of those men in the airport threatening to do the unthinkable. Or I might see Justin crying out for me as someone brutally ended his life. No. I mustn't close my eyes, even though they burned like hell.

I went into the bathroom and splashed cold water on my face. The whites of my eyes were red, making my normally pale blues appear electric. My wavy, blonde hair had certainly seen better days, too.

I laughed at myself. How inane to be worrying about my looks after that horribly fucked-up situation. *But you're intact, Mia. Nothing bad happened.* Thanks to King. And what had I done? Yelled at the guy. Okay, he was a cold-hearted, controlling man, but that didn't mean I should become him.

Just let it go. You can thank him later.

I returned to the cabin and hovered in the doorway of the cockpit. "So. How long is the flight to Villahermosa?"

Mack called back from his seat, "We're not going to Villahermosa. We're heading straight to Palenque. There's a small private airport there."

"Oh." My original flight had me going to Villahermosa, where King's email said I'd be "collected and transported to Palenque," like an object.

"King asked me to apologize about making you fly commercial, but he and I needed to be in Mexico City to take care of some business. We weren't sure what time things would wrap up," Mack yelled. "By the way, talking over my shoulder isn't my specialty. Why don't you come up front?"

For a second time that evening, I felt ashamed for my criticism of King. Apparently, he didn't mind sharing *some* things; he'd had a legitimate reason to put me on another flight. Had I misjudged him about other things, too?

Maybe. But it seemed easier to keep on hating him. If I started to soften towards him, where would that land me?

"You sure this is okay?" I peeked inside and held up my drink, wondering if it was safe near the equipment.

"Ah, I see you found the Macallan. King had me stock it just for you. He said you're a whisky girl; although he only has scotch—the good stuff."

Another gesture of thoughtfulness? At this rate, King might be out of the gutter and rated as an actual human being by day's end. But...how the hell did King know what I liked to drink? Had he been spying on me? Interviewing my friends?

I looked down at my glass. "Well, this is much better than the swill I usually drink," I said to make polite conversation.

Mack laughed. "For twelve thousand a bottle, I sure as hell hope so."

"Twelve thousand? I better sip slower, then."

"Don't worry. He's got a warehouse of that stuff he took as payment. He jokingly calls it the 'cheap stuff.'"

King joked? Another surprise. And I wish I'd known that King accepted liquor as payment. I could've said "no" to working for him and offered him a bottle of the "good stuff." Not that I'd be able to afford it. *Maybe he would have gone for some liquor-filled chocolates?*

"So," I took a sip of my drink and sat in the empty copilot seat, "how long have you worked for him?"

Mack flashed a glance my way. "A while."

"How did you meet?" I asked.

"You ask a lot of questions."

"Did King tell you about my brother?" I asked.

"Yes."

"Then can you really blame me?"

"No, I guess not."

"How do you know him?" I asked again.

Mack stared ahead, thinking before answering my question. "I needed something. He helped me."

All right. King had snagged Mack in a moment of desperation, too. "So once you had what you wanted, why didn't you just go?"

I knew my questions were forward, but I was in no mood to pretend or beat around the bush.

Mack shrugged his golden brows. "Not that I would, but no one reneges on a deal with King. No one. King takes every deal seriously. To the letter."

My heart thumped against my rib cage. "Meaning?"

Mack stroked the corners of his mouth. "Use your imagination."

I suppose I didn't have to. My gut already knew. It knew the first moment I'd laid eyes on King that he was not the sort of man who took deals lightly. He was cold and dangerous, and if you crossed him, he wouldn't hesitate to crush you. He'd basically said so, and I believed him.

"But if given the choice…" Mack was about to add something else, but stopped talking.

"What?"

"I guess if I could do it all over again, I would. King pays well. There is no bullshit agenda. And no one messes with you. Ever."

From the way Mack spoke, it sounded like he had an extreme amount of loyalty towards King. And once again, I found myself poking holes in my "King is a heartless devil" theory. That said, what was it that they did where "no one messing with you" was a perk of the job?

"But…who is he?" I asked.

Mack simply shrugged. "He's a businessman. He's also good at finding *stuff*. For a price."

I was beginning to grow tired of that explanation. "He hasn't found anything for me yet."

Mack laughed. "He will. Just give him time."

Time… It had been the one thing I'd watch slip through my fingers since I agreed to this arrangement. Justin was either dead or damned close to it. "I'm out of time."

And I could only ask myself one question: Why had I made this deal with King? Why? I'd given up everything—my dream job and, therefore, my home—and it had gotten me nowhere.

Because you were fucking desperate, Mia. There was no other choice.

CHAPTER SIX

After landing at a small airstrip surrounded by jungle somewhere outside the town of Palenque, a driver in a black SUV with tinted windows showed up to transport Mack and me to our accommodations for the night.

I asked the driver if he knew the address where my brother lived, thinking it would make sense to see if anything there could tell us more, but Mack quickly shut me down. "Trust me, King had people go through your brother's place with a fine-toothed comb weeks ago. If there was anything worth finding, he already found it."

What? I'd had the impression that King hadn't lifted a finger in three weeks beyond finding out about those phone calls.

"King also gave clear instructions to meet him tonight at the excavation site."

I looked at my watch. It was close to midnight already. "Tonight? Are you sure?"

"Yep." Mack didn't seem to think that was at all strange. "You have about an hour to rest, shower, eat, whatever. This car will be waiting for you."

I looked at the driver, a portly man with thick, curly, black hair who hadn't said a word to either of us. "Does he work for King?" I whispered.

Mack smirked. "You think King would leave you in the care of strangers?"

I had no idea what King would or wouldn't do.

"The answer is no, Mia," Mack clarified. "He is very protective of his possessions."

Possession? "I'm not his possession."

Mack didn't respond.

"I'm not."

Mack shook his head as if amused, but I chose not to get into a debate. They clearly lived by a different moral compass than my own.

Ten minutes later, the SUV pulled up to the hotel—a luxury resort with colorfully lit fountains and decorative pools, nestled in the jungle—where a bellhop in a tropical-print shirt immediately greeted us.

Mack slid out. "See you in the morning."

"Wait? Aren't you coming with me later?"

"I fly planes, and I do it better when I've had a little sleep." He winked and sauntered off.

I glanced back at the driver, who still faced forward. "Ummm…see you in about an hour?" I said to him.

The driver nodded.

Wow. Friendly.

The bellhop had extracted my small overnight bag from the back and waited for me. "Right this way, Miss Turner. Your room is ready."

I looked around at the open-aired lobby's fountains and beautiful floor-to-ceiling modern sculptures. I hoped King was paying for this place. I'd had the extreme pleasure of traveling extensively—Latin America, Asia, Europe—for work. I knew what five-star hotels cost, and King wasn't paying me. I was paying him. With my life.

He's the goddamned devil, I swear to God.

Well, someday this would all be over, and I'd get my life back. Someday. But today, I needed to play by his rules to save Justin.

Like one might expect to find in a five-star resort, my room was an oasis of doting comfort. Mini-bar fully stocked with nothing but reinforcements—aka, abundant whiskey—French milled soap, fluffy white robes and towels, and a large jet tub. And, also like one might expect, I didn't lie down on the king-sized bed to take a breather. Instead, I headed straight for the shower to wash away the smell of Guzman's cigarettes in my hair. *Disgusting pig. I hope King has you arrested.*

I turned up the hot water and let the forceful jets beat against my neck. I closed my eyes and inhaled the soothing scent of the lavender soap, pretending it was a magical potion that could erase any fear lurking inside my mind. But magic didn't exist. And soap couldn't do anything more than remove the dirt from my skin.

When I finally emerged from the bathroom, I found a large plate of bread, cheese, and fresh fruit laid out on the table. A card had been left beside the gleaming silverware.

Eat well. You will need your strength. – K

King had someone come into my room while I showered? I tightened the terrycloth belt around my waist and checked the deadbolt on the door. I hadn't locked it? I could've sworn I had.

You're tired, that's all. And yes, I was hungry, too.

I hovered over the freshly baked bread bundled in a cloth napkin. The warmth and aroma immediately triggered violent hunger pangs. I hadn't eaten since yesterday morning.

I sat and attacked the bread, smothering it with butter and thick creamy cheese. I moaned in culinary ecstasy as the salty, sweet fat melted away in my mouth.

Oh God. It couldn't possibly taste any better. There's something about the flavor of food when you're truly hungry that makes your taste buds feel like they're on steroids.

I grabbed another thick slice of bread and repeated the hedonistic act, piling on more butter and cheese. My eyes rolled in my head. *So good.*

So, so good. The only thing missing was a glass of wine.

I glanced over my shoulder, toward the mini-bar, thinking I could make due with whiskey; however, next to the flat-screen on the dresser was an uncorked bottle of champagne and an empty flute. *Oh. That'll do!* But why had he ordered champagne? Wasn't that more of a celebratory drink? Seemed a little strange, but it really did look delicious.

I popped from the chair and held up the bottle. It was French, obviously, and looked expensive, but I wasn't a big champagne connoisseur. I only drank it on special occasions or at parties.

I poured a glass and rolled the bubbles over my tongue. It was sweet and tart and delicious. "Oh, King, I think I love you."

I snorted at myself. *Yeah, right.* How could anyone love a man like that? Controlling, rude, cruel…The only redeeming quality I saw was his unfathomable good looks, which were instantly overshadowed by his barbaric shortcomings. I supposed some women might find his wealth attractive, too, but I wasn't one of them. Something about that man just wasn't right.

Yet, he still saved your ass tonight. That he had. I raised my glass into the air, mentally toasting to King. I would definitely thank him in person later. But how had he known where I was? How had we simply walked out of a secure area of an international airport? And what happened after I left?

I took another sip and mulled over the possibilities. Perhaps King was some international drug lord. That would explain his brute demeanor, his plane, and his connections at the airport. If that was so, why would he pimp himself out, rescuing people for money? That young receptionist who'd given me his number had told me that King saved her brother-in-law. That didn't seem like the kind of task a drug lord would bother with. Perhaps he was ex-CIA turned mercenary?

I looked at the clock. *Oh no.* I only had two minutes to get downstairs. I dug into my overnight bag and threw on some clothes. It wasn't even close to cold outside despite the time of year, so a tee, jeans, and tennis shoes seemed appropriate for whatever it was that I'd be doing.

Hell, what am I going to be doing? If King had already searched my brother's apartment, then wouldn't he have also covered the dig site? King didn't seem like the type to spend his time on anything if there wasn't a purpose to it, which meant he thought I could be of some use. But what? Why was I there?

At least you're doing something. And something was better than sitting behind that horrible desk, which gave me nightmares, wondering about Justin, waiting for him to call. Or worse, waiting to hear he was dead.

I scrambled to the elevator, down to the lobby, and outside, where the SUV waited.

I jumped in.

"You are late," said the driver. His accent didn't sound Mexican. More…Middle Eastern. "Mr. King doesn't appreciate tardiness."

"Uh. Sorry. I'll tell him it's not your fault."

The driver chuckled unappreciatively. "You think he will care?"

No, I guess I didn't. "Sorry." I squirmed in the leather seat, my mind spinning wildly with assumptions. What were we going to be looking for? What did King expect to find with me present that he couldn't find on his own? Regardless, I wasn't giving up the chance to learn something— anything.

"How far is the dig site?" I asked.

The driver shrugged. "About thirty minutes."

"Are we picking up King?" I figured he'd taken a later commercial flight. Unless…he had two jets?

Hmm…I thought it over. Maybe he did. It wouldn't surprise me. There was probably some minimum number of jets requirement for members of 10 Club.

"He is already there, waiting for you."

That was strange. King had left Mexico City after me, yet he was already at the dig site? I supposed it was possible considering I'd had an hour break. But why had he gone ahead?

My nerves kicked in, and I suddenly had the urge to turn around. What was I thinking traipsing around in the Mexican jungle at one a.m. in the morning? With King, no less. And Chiapas wasn't the safest of places even during the day. I'd lectured Justin about it several months ago when he'd taken the assignment. It was going to be his first time leading a team, and I was afraid his enthusiasm might make him overlook the safety factor. He assured me, however, that he'd done his homework. The local rebels, who called themselves *Zapatistas*, were no threat to anyone other than the government. "Fine. Then what about the drug traffickers?" I'd asked Justin. I'd done my fact-checking, too, and parts of Mexico were a warzone. People went missing all the time, especially anyone believed to have money.

"I'll be fine, Mia. I promise. Most of the issues are up north, and they're not interested in impoverished archaeologists."

"But you're so cute. I'm sure they'll make an exception." Like me, Justin had blond hair. Add those big green eyes and a sweet, goofy smile, he was instantly likeable.

Justin had laughed, and it had made me laugh, too. That was my favorite part about him. He had a kindness and levity that was infectious. "I promise I'll be fine."

Famous last words, Justin, I thought just as the SUV turned onto a dark, narrow dirt road that barely accommodated the large vehicle. Leaves slapped against the windows, causing me to flinch every time, but I was glad for the extra-large ride. The road was filled with deep potholes, muddy from a recent rain. Large rocks made navigating the terrain a slow, arduous task.

I leaned forward between the two front seats, trying to keep from getting carsick. "How much longer?"

"A few minutes."

I tried to imagine Justin coming over this road every day. I could just see his face filled with excitement that he might find some hidden stash of museum-worthy artifacts.

"Fucking buttons," I mumbled. Were they worth all this?

"Here we are." The driver pulled into a small turnout and handed me a flashlight.

"Where are we?" I'd expected to see a clearing with piles of dirt and an unearthed temple or something.

The driver pointed to the jungle in front of us. "There is a path. Follow it."

"But…" I blinked. "You're not expecting me to go alone, are you?"

He shrugged. "My job was to drive you here. Nothing more."

"Thanks a lot." I opened the door. The night air felt wetter and thicker out there than it had back at the hotel.

I looked up. There wasn't a single star in the sky. I turned on my flashlight and shined it toward the dense growth. A narrow opening had been cut away between two spindly trees.

I scratched my head. "You're sure King is waiting for me?"

The driver continued facing forward. "Yes."

"And you're not going anywhere until I come back?"

"No."

Shit. I didn't want to go out there alone, but…
"How far of a walk is it?"

I could practically hear the driver rolling his eyes.

"Never mind." I started down the path. My knees and hands trembled to the rhythm of my self-deprecating thoughts. I was a fool to be doing this. A stupid fool. But Justin was my brother, and I would do anything for him. Even this.

I ducked under stray branches and pushed forward, my ears on high alert for any sounds, human or otherwise. The narrow path bent to the right, around an enormous tree covered in twisted vines. The smell of damp earth filled my lungs, and it made me think about being buried alive.

Stop it, Mia. You're freaking yourself out.

A loud crunching of leaves stopped me in my tracks. I listened carefully and heard it again. The noise came from behind me.

"King?"

There was no reply, but the crunching became louder.

I picked up the pace. It was just an animal. It had to be. I began running, my frantic breaths making it difficult to take in the thick air. My foot hit a small pothole, and I went flying, face-first, into the mud. My flashlight dislodged from my death grip to land several feet in front of me.

I quickly picked myself up and glanced behind me. Two glowing orbs shined back.

"Fuck!" I scrambled my way over the muddy path as fast as I could go without tripping again. *Oh my God.* "King!" I screamed out. "King!"

I pushed through another dense wall of branches that lashed at my sweat-slicked skin and landed with another belly flop on the sticky ground. This time, I'd kept a hold on my flashlight, but when I lifted my head, I saw gray stone steps in front of me.

I shined my light up the face of the structure. *I know this place. I know this place.*

Something grabbed me from behind, and I let loose a bloodcurdling scream.

King's beautiful, cold eyes were inches from my nose. "Miss Turner, you're late."

I passed out.

CHAPTER SEVEN

I can't remember ever fainting before, but if given the chance to waltz over fiery coals from the pits of hell or faint in the midst of a horrifying situation, I'd take the coals. Because what they don't tell you about fainting is that waking back up feels like having your brain scraped off the side of the road after being run over by a semi.

When my throbbing skull allowed me to open my eyes, my consciousness popped on like a light bulb. "Shit!" I sat up and immediately recognized where I was: my hotel room. The thick curtains were cracked open and a powerful beam of sunlight shined across the foot of the bed. I looked down at my body. I wore only my pink underwear and bra.

"Nice of you to join us, Miss Turner."

I gasped. King sat in the corner of the room, his legs comfortably crossed, and his back to the unopened portion of the blackout curtains.

"What the hell is going on?" My chest heaved with panic.

He tipped his head to one side and smirked. "Just sitting here, enjoying the view."

Although his face wasn't in full sunlight, I saw his eyes scanning my nearly naked torso.

"Don't," I fumed. "Don't you dare play stupid with me."

He didn't respond, but he didn't stop checking me out either. *Bastard.*

I stood and went over to the closet for a robe. *Son of a bitch.*

"Whatever happened last night," I called out, "you'd better start explain—" I turned with the robe in my hand, and King was right there, inches from my body. His piercing gaze drilled down, halting all thoughts in my brain.

"I'd better what?" He rubbed the thick, black stubble on his chin as if contemplating something immoral.

King didn't wear his normal garb, but instead had on a well-fitting, black T-shirt that showcased every hard curve of his chest and upper arms. His jeans were no different in terms of illuminating the powerful muscles comprising his lower torso.

"Like what you see, Mia?"

"Huh?" My eyes snapped back to his face, but I couldn't seem to focus on anything other than the sensuality of this man, especially those sinful lips and hypnotic eyes with shimmering silver highlights.

"I will take that as a yes," he said in a low, deep voice.

I nodded, but didn't know why. I didn't want him. I didn't. He was cruel and scary and—

He gripped my waist and spun us both around, planting my ass on the dresser. He grabbed a handful of my hair and pulled my head back to stare possessively into my eyes.

I wasn't scared, but I couldn't move. I couldn't think. I just knew I suddenly wanted him to do what he was doing.

He slowly dipped his head, and when his lips pushed against mine, I closed my eyes and relished the roughness of his kiss. He plunged his tongue between my lips, and I opened my mouth to him. The kiss was dangerous and dark. It was claiming and brutal. It pounded its way right through me, sending a hard heat charging between my legs.

I couldn't get enough.

Suddenly, the man I was kissing felt like a different version of him. A version that was driven by passion and heart. A version that was powerful and determined, but never cruel.

I pushed my fingers through his black hair and savored the soft thickness of it. I slid my hands down to his broad shoulders and then glided them over the hard mounds of his pecs. God, he was so perfect.

I slipped my arms around him and pulled him closer, thinking about how I wanted our bodies to do what they were meant to.

Slowly, his hands journeyed over my breasts to my hips, down to my knees, where he jerked my legs open and slid his body between them.

"I'm going to break you, Miss Turner."

My eyes jarred open, but it wasn't King standing intimately between my thighs. It was a beast with black eyes and translucent skin.

I screamed.

"Nice of you to join us, Miss Turner."

Panting, my eyes darted from side to side. *Ceiling.* I was looking at a ceiling.

"Oh my God." *What happened?* I sat up. I was on the bed in my hotel room, fully clothed and covered in dried mud. Only the very edges of the comforter remained a pristine white. The rest was as filthy as I was. I looked at the clock on the nightstand. It was one in the afternoon.

Then I glanced at King, who sat in the exact same corner of the room as I'd just dreamed about. But had it been a dream? I felt violated and rabid. I felt like he'd been inside my head and my body, and I wanted to scratch the bastard's eyes out.

I lunged for King, but he had more than enough time to react. He threw me to the hard tile floor, knocking the wind from my lungs. I gulped for air and swung with my fists. He lunged on top of me and pinned my arms above my head. I wiggled and flailed. I wanted to kill him.

"Mia, you will calm yourself," he snarled in my ear, "or I will do it for you."

My breath returned to my body, and I sucked in the much-needed air. "Fuck you, King."

"I thought we established that you are not my type. Though, perhaps I could be persuaded."

Ugh! I fought to free my arms, but he simply laughed while the weight of his body crushed me.

"Get off me!"

"Trust me, I have far better things to do than quell a temper tantrum." His lips twitched. He seemed to be enjoying this.

I stilled and feigned calmness.

"You think I don't know that trick?" he scoffed. "I can feel the frenetic pace of your heart against my chest. But you're much weaker than I, Mia. I'll have you back on the floor before you bat an eyelash the wrong way."

I closed my eyes and tried not to think about the weight of his body pressing into me or that those intimate parts I'd just dreamed of were only separated by my muddy clothes and whatever he wore.

"We'll stay here all day, if need be," he cautioned. "However, if you continue to wiggle, you may trigger involuntary responses in my lower extremities."

Damn him!

"By the way, just why are you so angry, Miss Turner?"

"Where do I start?" I growled.

"At the beginning." Once again, his lips twitched, flashing a devious smile.

"Get. Off. Me."

"As you wish," he said, "but if you attack me again, I will not be so gentle. Although," he paused for effect, "I am beginning to wonder if gentle is what you want."

He rolled off, and I caught my breath. When I sat up, he was once again seated in the dark corner, calmer than an early morning breeze.

"Now, Miss Turner—"

"What happened last night?" I demanded.

"You fainted. I brought you here."

"Is that all?" I asked.

He shrugged his dark, silky brows. "What do you think happened?"

I looked away. Okay. Maybe that sexual episode had been just a dream—a relief—but there was still the matter of everything else.

I rallied a bit of courage and met his intimidating stare head on. "Why did you bring me to Palenque, King?"

"Because I wanted to."

"Enough!" Of course, my anger only seemed to amuse him. "You promised to help me find Justin, but you made me sit in that empty office for three weeks. Then you dragged me to the jungles of Mexico in the middle of the night, only to scare the shit out of me."

My mind quickly flashed back to that ruin from the previous night. *Wait.* I did know it. The damned thing was the Temple of the Cross. Justin had sent pictures of it, and it was a well-known tourist attraction.

Not Justin's dig site...Oh Lord. I covered my face. *King is just messing with me.*

"You brought me here to see how far you could push me, didn't you?" I seethed.

He leaned forward in his chair and rested his forearms over the tops of his thighs. That's when I noticed he wore jeans and a black T-shirt. A leather cuff, with several small buckles and about three inches wide, obscured most of his tattoo.

"You think I have time for petty games, Miss Turner? I brought you here because we have work to do."

"What work?"

He stood and crossed the small distance to where I sat on the floor. "Get up."

I didn't like staring at his knees—made me feel like I was groveling —so I did what he asked. "I'm up, King. Now what?"

The man moved like a hungry viper and gripped my wrist. The veins in his muscular arms bulged with tension.

"Ow!" I tried to pull away, but he had the strength of ten vices. He flipped over my left wrist to expose the tender underside. I looked down at a black circle with the letter "K" boldly written in script in the center. The pale flesh was raised and red, like a fresh scrape.

"You tattooed me?"

"It's for your own protection."

"Are you insane?"

He leaned down to whisper in my ear. "What would you like me to say, Mia? That I own you? Every inch of you? That even those dark spaces inside your head belong to me? Because they do. You are mine now."

Oh my god. Oh my god. He's the devil. He's got to be. I yanked my arm away, fully aware that he'd permitted me to do so. Otherwise, I wouldn't have gotten free. "Why would you do this to me?"

"Because, Miss Turner, it was necessary. And whether you like it or not, you no longer live in your naïve little world filled with designer heels, fancy lunches, and highlighted hair. It's time to open your eyes."

"Why? So I can see you're an evil, sadistic prick who enjoys controlling me?"

He casually strode to the door and actually seemed offended. "*You* came looking for *me*. *You* asked for my help. And *you* are here because you want to be. The issue appears to be your willingness to admit the truth to yourself." He yanked open the door, allowing the sunlight to pour inside the room.

"The *truth* is simple; I'm here because I want to find Justin."

He dipped his head. "And so we shall. I'll send the driver at ten tonight. Until then, I suggest you rest. You'll need your strength." He paused. "And, Mia, don't be late this time."

King left my hotel room, but he didn't leave my head. The rage flowed through me like hot shards of glass.

"A tattoo? A tattoo?" *What the fuck?*

Calm down, Mia. You can get it removed. But what sort of psycho chases a woman in the jungle and then tattoos his initial on her wrist?

The same sort who's been playing mind games, manipulating you from day one.

The room began to spin, bright colors blotching my vision. I ran into the bathroom and threw up. Luckily, there wasn't much there.

God, this is so messed up. I hung my head in my hands. I couldn't allow this to go on; torturing was not part of the deal. And King's psycho power trips, which he claimed were for my own protection, had gone too far. But the fact was, it was my fault. I'd been allowing all this to go on. I'd been letting him get inside my head and control me.

Dammit! What's the matter with you, Mia? I knew I'd been in a fragile state when I agreed to this twisted relationship, but how could I have been so completely blind? King wasn't going to help me nor had he ever intended to. He simply saw me as a desperate woman he could take advantage of to fulfill his demented, sadistic urges.

Why the hell had it taken me so long to see the truth?

I almost laughed. Almost. But I couldn't. My stupidity wasn't funny. What was funny was that I'd initially been worried about King being a conman. Right now, I'd almost be grateful if he was. At least conmen ruin your life in the pursuit of something I could understand: they wanted money. But King played with people's lives just to get off.

And that dream? What was that about? I could never be attracted to a man who wasn't good or compassionate. King was neither. *But that dream…*I remember feeling like he was someone completely different. Still powerful, but kind and passionate. Not cold and ruthless.

It was just a dream, Mia. Don't start hoping the man is something he's not.

I paced the room several times. *What am I going to do?* I had to blow the whistle on this insanity immediately, but I couldn't abandon Justin, so I'd just have to start finding answers on my own. And if King threatened me, then I'd go to the police. That was about all I *could* do.

"I'm done with you, King. Done," I mumbled to myself.

I jumped in the shower and washed the mud from my hair and face. I threw on clean jeans and a blue T-shirt, then headed out to grab a cab. I wanted to see what was in my brother's apartment and, perhaps, get some answers of my own.

I am taking control of this goddamned nightmare.

CHAPTER EIGHT

When the cab pulled up to the stucco building sandwiched between a crowded *taquería* blaring salsa music and a barbershop, it struck me as odd that I wouldn't recognize my own brother's home. The narrow structure had two garage doors on the first floor and two floors of apartments above, each with private balconies overlooking the street.

I walked up the outside stairs to apartment one, my brother's, and buzzed the door. There was an iron security gate, but it had been left open. After a few seconds, I knocked, too.

No answer.

I crossed my arms and thought for a moment. Perhaps the upstairs neighbor had a key or could put me in touch with the landlord. I marched upstairs, but no one was home there either.

Shit. I'd have to come back later.

I passed Justin's apartment on the way down, and I don't know what possessed me, but I jiggled the handle. It was open.

"Hello?" I pushed the door and peeked inside the living room. There were two off-white couches facing a television, and an open kitchen with a breakfast bar. The place was tidy and undisturbed, at least from what I could see of it.

I stepped inside and smelled the air. It was stale and dank, like it hadn't been aired out in a while.

"Hello?"

I walked through the living room, down a dark hallway leading to three doors. The first was the bathroom, also spotless. The second had to be his roommate's—the desk was clean, and the bed had a plaid comforter. My brother hated plaid, and he'd never had a clean desk a day in his life. When we were little, it was always littered with his latest dinosaur models or piles of rocks he collected in the yard. To my knowledge, he hadn't changed that habit.

I opened the final door and tried not to cry. On the nightstand, next to a huge pile of papers and books, sat a photo of Justin and me smiling together at Thanksgiving last year. It was one of those rare occasions in recent years where he and I were both able to make it. One of us was usually halfway across the globe for work. That was why my parents had made such a huge deal and taken the picture.

I grabbed the photo and stared at the thing. "Where in the world are you, baby brother?"

"Who are you?"

I jumped. "Oh, God." The guy had on a short-sleeved, burgundy and blue plaid shirt and khaki shorts. His brown eyes were the same shade as his short brown hair.

"Not God. Brian," he said. "And you are?"

"Oh. Sorry." I extended my hand. "I'm Mia, Justin's sister."

His hand was ice cold, like he'd just come from a meat locker, and I noticed a tribal tattoo snaking up his forearm. It was of a pickax and a skull.

"College," he said.

"Sorry?"

"I got the tattoo in college." He flashed a goofy smile. Yeah, I could see Justin and him living together.

"It's an interesting design." I wasn't about to show him mine. How could I possibly explain it?

"No, it's not. I got drunk at a frat party—we were all really into archaeology. That's how I met Justin and started working with him."

"You worked with my brother?" Justin had only mentioned sharing an apartment with another American.

"What? Did he fire me?" Brian said jokingly.

"No. I meant—well, I thought his entire crew had been...involved." I didn't want to say kidnapped or murdered. I was sure the wounds were still raw. "How did you...avoid—you know?"

Brian frowned. "What are you talking about?"

"The incident at the dig site?"

"Are you sure you're Justin's sister?"

"Yeah." I held up the photo.

Brian crossed his arms. "I'm not aware of any incident."

"The entire crew is missing."

He looked at me as if I were completely mad. "No, they're not. I was just over there. Everything's fine."

My head started to spin. "But I got a call from the embassy—wait. When's the last time you saw Justin?"

Brian's eyes flashed at the ceiling. "This morning; he said he needed to go Villahermosa to pick up supplies. He'll be back tomorrow."

That's impossible.

"Where did you see him?" My heart pounded ferociously.

"Here."

"Are you sure?" I asked.

"Someone's been messing with you, Mia."

But Justin hadn't called me in weeks. And the last time we had spoken, he said not to come looking for him.

"You okay?" he asked.

"I just don't understand," I mumbled to myself.

"Justin has a pretty twisted sense of humor sometimes."

No, he didn't. He was sweet and kind. "He would never play this kind of joke, especially on me." I paused and mulled it over. Something wasn't right. I'd had men break into my hotel room. I'd been detained and threatened at the airport. I hadn't imagined that. "Did Justin mention anything? Problems with the local officials? Threats? Anything?"

Brian shook his head. "Nothing. And we're always careful when we find something valuable."

Valuable? "Like what? Gold?"

Brian chuckled. "Not that valuable. But we find some pretty cool stuff, worth a lot on the black market. The moment we unearth anything, it's catalogued, registered with the local government and the insurance company, and—if precious enough—placed in a vault at the bank until we know which museum or university it's going to."

"So no one's robbed you guys or threatened anyone?" I asked.

"No. Lucky us, I guess."

I just couldn't believe this. I felt like I was in the midst of some bizarre conspiracy.

My wobbly legs were no longer able to hold my weight, so I sat on the bed. "You're sure Justin is okay? Because I called his cell phone; he's not answering."

"Maybe he lost it again. The guy loses everything. Are you sure you're all right?"

I nodded and willed my legs to stand again. "Yeah. I'm just…" I didn't know the right word; confused wouldn't cut it. "Tell Justin I need to talk to him. Immediately." I jotted down the hotel's name on a slip of paper from Justin's desk. "I'm staying here. The moment you see him, have him call my cell."

"Uh, okay. Are you *sure* you're all right?" He looked very uncomfortable.

If Justin's crew wasn't missing and Brian had seen my brother only hours ago, then could it be possible? Was someone messing with me? Or was I being scammed? Used? Going mad?

"No. I'm actually not okay. Not even close. Just have him call me." I headed out to the street to hail a cab back to the hotel. I needed to talk to King.

⊹⊱⊰⊹

"What do you mean there's no King?" I fumed at the poor hotel desk clerk. I knew she didn't deserve to be treated like crap, but I apparently had no other setting than "major bitch" at the moment. "He has to be here."

She shook her head. "I'm sorry, ma'am, but there's no one here with that last name."

"Are you sure?"

"I can check under his first name. What is it?"

I groaned. I'd never even bothered to ask King his full name. "I don't know. He just goes by..." I threw up my hands, "King. That's it."

"I'm sorry, Miss Turner, I cannot help you."

I was about to shuffle away in defeat but... "He's paying for my room. Isn't there a name?"

The woman's dark brown eyes returned to her screen as she tapped away on the keyboard. "Ummm...no. Your room is being billed to K Enterprises."

"Do you have any other guests registered under that company?"

She did a quick search. "Only you and another gentleman, but his name is not King."

"A Mack something?" I guessed. Why didn't I know his name, either? What was it with me and not knowing names?

She hesitated, then nodded.

"Ugh. Where is that psycho?" I smacked my palm on the counter and realized I was the one who sounded psycho.

I forced a smile onto my lips. "Thank you—I mean...*gracias*."

She bowed her head. "*Para servirle, señorita.*"

I'd have to confront King later. And when I did, I'd tell him our deal was off. He could make any threats he liked, but this sick little game was over. *Screw King.*

I trudged my way up to my suite to get my stuff. I would just go back to Justin's and wait for him to show.

Once inside, I grabbed my bag and collected my things from the bathroom, but when I bent over to grab the muddy clothes I'd left on the floor, a dizzy spell nearly toppled me. I stumbled my way to the bed and flopped down, closing my eyes. I hadn't been eating or taking care of myself. And don't get me started on the stress.

But you're fine now, Mia. Just relax. Everything is going to be okay. Justin wasn't dead or in trouble. Brian had seen my brother only this morning, and there'd been no assault on the crew.

I sighed with relief, because, whatever crap was happening, Justin was okay. The rest would be okay, too.

"Miss Turner, what the *fuck* are you doing?"

I popped up on my elbows and found King's large, imposing figure, dressed in that same black tee and jeans, hovering over me.

"How did you get in here?" I asked.

"I have a key," he growled. "Didn't I warn you about being late? You think this is some fucking joke?"

Late? I glanced at the clock on the nightstand. 10:02? "I-I don't know what—"

"Get your ass up, Miss Turner. Naptime is over."

I swung my legs over the edge of the bed and planted my feet on the floor. How in the world was it already ten at night? When I'd closed my eyes, it couldn't have been any later than three.

I began massaging my temples to soothe the ache inside my skull.

"Now, Miss Turner," King commanded in a low, restrained voice.

I held out my hand. "Stop. Okay? Just—"

Before I could say another word, King had me by the shoulders and plastered against the wall. "I'll stop when I'm damned good and ready."

"No." I shook my head. "Whatever game you're playing ends now. I'm done."

"You think this is a game, Mia?"

Mia. Why did I feel like he always used my first name as a weapon? *Another one of his bullshit, mind-game moves.*

"Yeah," I replied bitterly. "Justin is alive and well. There was no attack on his team."

King's brows furrowed. "Where did you go today?"

"Where did *you* go today?" I asked simply to piss him off.

Rage flickered in his striking silvery eyes, but I didn't crumble.

"Justin is alive, and our deal is off." I squirmed against him, but he was just too damned strong.

The hard, angry line of King's lips suddenly twitched and then softened as if he were listening to a joke. A joke I wasn't privy to. He placed the barrel of his fist over his mouth and smothered a snide chuckle.

"What's so funny?"

He released me and backed away. "Once again, you. You, Miss Turner."

He was insane. Insane and evil. So why did I care so much about what he thought?

"Your brother may be alive, but he is not well. And neither is his crew."

"I just saw his roommate," I argued. "I was at his apartment."

King nodded. "I'm sure you were."

"And?"

"And we're leaving," he said.

"I'm not going anywhere with you."

"Then I will have Mack fly you back to San Francisco tonight. And when you get there, you will learn the truth."

"Which is?" I asked.

"I am right. And by the time you realize what a jackass you've been, it will be too late for your brother."

"Justin is here, safe and alive. I'm not leaving without seeing him."

King grinned once again as if he knew something I didn't and my behavior was the world's most amusing joke. "Very well, Miss Turner. I had hoped to do things my way—the easier, less painful way. But I see you've made up your mind and any efforts to shield you will only further convince you that I am a," his smile stretched wider, "demon from hell." He moved toward the door. "Go see your brother. And once you've gotten your pissy little ego under control, we'll resume."

I growled at him as he shut the door. *Resume?* We weren't *resuming* anything. As far as I was concerned, my deal with King was null and void. I found Justin, not King. And if King had bothered to lift a finger, he would have known Justin was never missing. That didn't mean some other weird crap wasn't going on, but it wasn't King's concern. And neither was I. Not anymore.

Less than thirty minutes later, I was back at my brother's apartment. I knocked on the door, but again, there was no answer. I tried the handle. "Still unlocked?" These guys were begging to get robbed, but when I reached to flip on the lights, nothing happened. I stepped to the side and allowed the light from the outside stairwell to illuminate the entryway. Garbage and broken glass lay everywhere.

"What the hell?" I whispered.

"*Señorita. Que hace aquí?*"

I jumped and clutched the fabric over my chest. "Oh my God. You scared the crap out of me."

The man, perhaps in his fifties, wearing dark running shorts and a Puma T-shirt, stared at me.

"Do you speak English?" I asked.

"No. No, English. *Usted no debe de estar aquí.*"

Crap. "Uhhh…" I pointed inside the apartment. "*Mi hermano.* Justin. Have you seen him?" I pointed to my eyes. "*Ver. Mi hermano?*" I knew my Spanish sucked, but it was the best I could do.

The man waved both hands in front of me. "*No. No lo he visto por un chingo.*"

"*Chingo?*" I didn't understand. "Uhhh…*cuanto?*" I tapped my watch. "*Cuanto* time?"

He nodded. "*Más que un mes.*"

Un mes. I knew those words. They meant "one month."

I blinked and felt my blood pressure dropping. This couldn't be right. "Ummm. How long…*cuanto?*" I pointed inside. "*Cuanto* like this? *Basura.*" *Basura* meant garbage.

"*Un mes, señorita.*" He held out his index finger for emphasis.

That couldn't be right.

"*Yo vivo, arriba,*" he said and then pointed to the apartment above. He lived upstairs?

Shit. No. "This is wrong. *No correcto.*"

He held up his finger once again, but to ask me to wait. He slipped his phone from his pocket, tapped away at the screen, and then held it up. "*Ya vez. Aquí es el reporte que salió en el periódico.*"

I glanced at the tiny screen. It was a photo of this apartment building on the website *Noticias De Palenque*. The header said *Secuestrado, Cinco Arqueólogos Americanos*, or Five Archaeologists Kidnapped. There was a tiny photo of each man, including my brother and...

"Fuck." I nearly fainted. The other face I recognized was Brian's.

I covered my mouth. What was happening? "Uhhh, *gracias*." I stumbled down the steps to the street, and there, waiting, was a black SUV. The rear passenger-side window lowered, and I immediately recognized those thick black lashes and mesmerizing eyes punching through the darkness.

I tried to keep from throwing up.

"Now do you believe me, Miss Turner?"

I couldn't move. I didn't know what to believe. I wanted to scream. I wanted to pull my hair out from the roots. *This is what it feels like to be in hell*, I thought.

King slipped from the vehicle and approached me, but I held out my hands, warning him not to come closer. Then the tears began to pour from my eyes, and I had to use my hands to cover the horrifying scream that erupted from my mouth.

I was certain that King was going to slap me or throw me into the car to keep me from drawing the attention of passersby, but instead, he pulled me against his hard frame. He held my head to his broad chest and stroked my hair while I sobbed hysterically for five whole seconds. I suddenly felt safe, so incredibly safe. Like nothing could touch me or hurt me ever again. Except for King.

He gripped my shoulders and pushed me back, pinning me with his hypnotic, jewel-like eyes. "That's enough crying, Miss Turner. We have work to do."

I blinked at him. "You *are* the devil, aren't you?" How else could I explain what he knew or how I saw things that couldn't possibly be real? He was messing with my mind.

He looked at me oddly and smirked with those exquisite lips. "I would gladly take the position if it were up for grabs and actually existed."

I stared, not amused one bit.

He gave my shoulder a little squeeze. "If I were the devil, then why would I be helping you?"

"Who *are* you?" I asked.

He shrugged his sable brows. "I, Miss Turner, am the man who can find anything. And you…" He gripped my wrist, flipped it over, and then pointed to the "K" tattooed on my arm. "Are my Seer of Light. Let's hope you stay alive longer than the last one." He turned away and got into the waiting SUV.

I stood there shaking, wondering what on God's green earth he'd meant.

He looked at me from inside the vehicle. "Are you getting in? Or do I have to drag you?"

I didn't know who I was, where I was, or what was happening, let alone what else to do, so I got in.

"Close the door, Miss Turner," King instructed.

I did as he asked.

"Very good." He glanced up at the driver. "Arno, take us to the dig site."

As if my brain had been set to slow motion, drugged with a strong sedative, I turned my head toward King. Still dressed in his dark jeans, he now wore a long-sleeved, black T-shirt and black boots. His jet black hair was messier than usual and falling a bit in his face like he'd just towel-dried it and left it that way. He looked fierce and untamed, yet regal and shockingly handsome. He exuded potent, raw, male energy. "Are you staring, Miss Turner?"

I nodded absently, only able to feel the tips of my fingers and the tops of my toes. I think I was in shock.

"Like what you see?" he asked.

Had he really just asked that? The exact same words he'd used in my dream?

I blinked. "What's a Seer of Light?"

He looked ahead at the road. "You'll understand once we get there, but it is a sixth sense very few have. That is why I brought you to the temple last night, to borrow some of its power to help you unleash yours. And to mark you."

The temple has power? He used it on me? Why do I feel so wooooozy? Maybe King planned to murder me tonight and had doped me up.

"What happened to the last Seer again?" I said with a slow slur.

"She died because she disobeyed me."

Holy crap. I knew it. "You killed her, didn't you?"

King flashed an irritated look. "No. I needed her, just like I need you. To do your job for me." He shifted his body in my direction and rested his thick arm along the back of the seat.

"What's happening to me?" I asked.

"You're waking up, Mia. You're seeing the truth."

The truth? I knew that word, but my mind felt all slushy inside.

"What did you do to me?" I mumbled. "Did you drug me?"

"It's simply your brain trying to reconcile the old reality with the new. It will wear off. Why don't you try humming since that seems to help you?"

He knew that I hummed? How odd. I closed my eyes. "I feel dizzy."

King slipped his hand from the back of the chair onto my thigh and gave it a rub. His touch felt strangely sensual. It was tingly and electric. I liked it.

"You'll be fine," he said in that deep, deep voice that sounded like it had been cut from a blanket woven from thick dark chocolate and sin.

I snorted with drunken amusement. "Chocolate blankets. Ha! Okaaaay."

"Rest, Miss Turner. We'll be there soon."

I mumbled some sort of agreement and drifted off to images of Justin, Brian, and King swirling in my head like a fuzzy kaleidoscope.

When I opened my eyes again, it took several moments for my vision to clear. I wiggled my way upright in the backseat, rubbing my tingly face.

"King is waiting for you below."

I shook my head. "Huh?"

The driver—*Arno?*—pointed to my side of the vehicle. Once again, the night was pitch black, but I could make out a mound of dirt a few yards away.

"Oh—kee—do—kee." I stumbled from the SUV. I felt like I'd downed a bottle of tequila, then rum, then whiskey. I dropped to my hands and knees, retching, but nothing came out.

The driver came to my aid and pulled me up. "You'll be fine, Miss Turner."

"Yes. Yes. I'm okay. I'm okay." *I think...?*

He showed me to a wooden ladder that led to a dark hole in the ground. "Turn around."

I did as Arno instructed and clumsily lowered myself until I reached solid footing.

"Ah, Miss Turner, you are awake. How do you feel?" King's strong arms gripped my waist to steady me. I felt wobbly and disoriented, but I liked the feel of his powerful hands digging into me.

"Like Alice," I replied.

King's lips twitched in that special way that almost looked like a smile. "Yes, and here is your rabbit hole."

Gas lanterns and candles illuminated much of the dark space, but all I saw were the dirt floor, dirt walls, and dirt overhead.

"Is this it?" I asked.

King took my hand, and I noticed how his touch was hot and cold all at the same time. And it did things to me. It made my blood flow faster, made me breathe heavier. It worked its way inside my mind and pushed against it. His touch felt almost…erotic.

"This is where your brother was searching for it."

"Searching for what?" I asked.

"I don't know. But it was powerful. Can you feel its energy, Miss Turner, radiating through the rocks and ground we stand upon?"

I only felt him, his touch, moving inside my body. I wanted more.

I wiggled my head back and forth. Why did I feel so loopy? Why couldn't I think straight? "I feel like throwing up."

King placed his hands on either side of my face, which only increased the wild, erotic sensations pulsing through me. "Mia." He stroked the hair from my eyes. "You are safe now. You simply need to relax, to let your mind do the work. Do you understand?"

Safe? With King? Impossible. I'd never be safe around him.

I nodded anyway.

"Good," he said. "Now look around, and tell me what you see."

I wanted to please him. I wanted to do exactly what he asked. I just didn't want him to stop touching me. "I see…I see…dirt?" I looked back into his eyes. They were no longer silver, but black, black like the night.

"Try again, Mia. Try harder." His hands moved to my shoulders and massaged gently.

I closed my eyes and fully leaned my mind into the sensual power of his touch. *I am stoned. Stoned. I think I like it. No, I don't. I like control. I like to know what's going on.* "And I like you, King. I like you." I poked his chest. "You're sexy and big, and I…like you."

Had I said that? Me?

King sighed. "If only that were true. Now focus, Mia."

"Okaaay. But you have to kiss me again. Then I'll do anything you want."

"Again?"

"Like you did in my dream."

"So you dream about me?" The thought seemed to please him.

"Yes or no, King. Yes or no," I said, mocking his voice.

Hesitation flickered in his striking eyes, but then those full carnal lips edged with thick black stubble smiled at me, and I melted.

"Just remember, *you* asked." He threaded his fingers through my hair and cautiously brought his mouth to mine.

Oh God. I sucked in a sharp breath through my nose. His kiss shot delicious tingles and sparks through my entire body. It made my stomach quiver and twist and…

I leaned my drunken weight into that sublimely masculine body forged from solid muscle and cold, hard, domineering strength. This wasn't the taste of a man who was damaged or evil, but of a man who conquered and triumphed. This man felt like a god.

I sighed and savored the sensation of his hot, unrelenting lips roughly pressed to mine and of his hot tongue sliding in and out of my mouth. I slipped my arms around his tight waist and pulled his warm body closer, only to feel the pang of rejection as he pushed me back.

"No, Miss Turner. I gave you what you wanted, and now you must reciprocate."

I made a pouty sigh. "Fine. But…wait. What did you want?"

King's dark eyes washed over the room. "Tell me what you see."

I held up my index finger. "Ah, yes!"

I surveyed the perfectly rectangular cavern with crudely cut wooden beams supporting the ceiling, surprised to see all sorts of colors swirling in various spots over the dirt floor. "Woooow. I see colors. Lots of pretty, pretty colors," I slurred.

"Do you see anything red?" King asked.

"Yes!" I pointed to several large spots on the ground. There were four.

"Very good. And do you see anything with a black and red pattern?" he asked.

"Right there." I pointed to a shallow hole in the corner. "It has a weird design. Kind of like crisscrosses." It reminded me of something, but I couldn't think of what.

I turned to King. "What is it?"

King's eyes lit with unfiltered joy. "It is the Artifact—where it used to lie, anyway."

"Artifact?"

Suddenly, my head felt like it was buried beneath ten tons of gravel, like something wanted to press me into the ground and send me to the fiery pits of hell. I stumbled and gripped the sides of my head.

"Fight to accept it, Miss Turner. You must fight."

I grimaced in pain. "Fight...what?"

He didn't answer. Instead, he asked me a question. "Where do you see the red?"

I pointed to one of the four spots only three feet away.

"Dig, Miss Turner."

My mind was beginning to clear, the lucidity returning. "Dig?"

King pointed to the loose dirt. "Dig."

"Why?" I asked.

Yes, my head is becoming clearer now. Why am I here?

Regardless of what my mind said, my body lowered itself to the ground and began to dig. Three or four inches down, I hit something soft. I scooped several handfuls of earth to the side, then brushed away the remaining dirt. It was an arm.

I jumped up and screamed.

King gripped me firmly from behind. "Look at it. I don't want there to be any doubts moving forward of what is real and what is not."

I twisted my head away. "No, I can't."

"If you want to find your brother, you will look." He pushed my jaw in the direction of the hole. "Open your eyes, Mia."

I couldn't help myself from doing what he asked. When my eyes registered what I saw, I understood something profoundly disturbing; I was not right in the head.

"That's…that's…" The arm had a tattoo of a serpent and a pickax. The flesh was rotten and blue. "It's Brian," I cried. *Oh God.* "Is Justin here, too?" *No. Please, Lord, no!*

"He is not, Miss Turner. Those others are your brother's missing crew."

I crumpled beneath the weight of my own body.

CHAPTER NINE

London.
A Few Days Later.

"You need to eat, Mia." Mack lifted my head from
the pillow and tipped a bowl of broth toward my
mouth, but I refused to drink. Frustrated, he
grumbled under his breath before placing the bowl
on the nightstand. "Do you want King to put my
head on a spike?"

I glared at his blue, puppy-dog eyes. "Don't you
have a plane to fly or something?" I tucked the
covers tightly under my arms and closed the gap of
my white robe. I felt so damned cold.

"Thanks to you, no, I don't." He swept his hand
over his body to point out his outfit. He wore
regular old khakis and a green-colored, Irish wool
turtleneck, which meant he wasn't flying today, I
guessed.

"Not my fault King made you the official Mia-
sitter."

Mack shook his head. "It is, and you know it."

Okay. Maybe it was. When I woke up a few days ago with no recollection of traveling to this posh London hotel with a view of the marble arch, I was sicker than a dog on a teacup ride. King had said it was a side effect of my "gift," but that didn't matter. I had jumped from the bed and, apparently, tried to kill him with my bare hands. I don't remember the incident, but according to Mack, I told King I would slice off his balls with a rusty hacksaw if I ever saw him again. I guess that's when I told him to get Mack, the only person I could stand to look at without vomiting and who King would trust my care to.

I shrugged. "Maybe. But why the hell are we even here? Did King find a record of Justin getting on a flight?"

"No." Mack shook his head. "Would you just eat?"

"I'm not hungry." I still felt like I had the stomach flu. I'd been able to hold down water and juice. That was it.

"You'll feel better once you eat something."

As if feeling better is even possible. The crazy crap I'd seen in Palenque guaranteed I wouldn't.

I scoffed and looked away. "Is that what King told you?"

"No. It's basic biology. Your body needs food." He let loose a throaty grumble. "Mia, I fully understand why you're upset; however, may I share something with you?"

I knew Mack wasn't my friend, but there was something about him that made me want to trust him.

"Are you going to tell me who King really is or what he did to me?" I asked.

Mack shoved his fingers through his disheveled blond hair. "No. King will tell you what you need to know. And to be frank, I don't know as much as you think. I just know he's—"

"What? Satan? A vampire who walks in daylight?"

"No. But," he gave me a disapproving look, "Satan? Vampires? How old are you, eight?"

Who could blame me for reaching towards the impossible in search of answers? The things I'd seen, the things I'd felt—there were no logical explanations. "King practically asked for my soul in exchange for finding my brother. Which he still hasn't done."

"Why do you think he brought you to London, Mia?" Mack stood up. "The sooner you start eating, the sooner you'll be able to resume the search. But King made it clear that you're not leaving this room until you've straightened out. He doesn't want you getting hurt."

King didn't care about me, so why would Mack say that? And it hadn't gotten past me that Mack had done the old switcheroo and changed topics.

"Can you at least tell me, is he dangerous?"

Mack coughed out a laugh. "What the hell do you think?"

I nodded.

"Then you'd be right. So, are you going to eat?"

"Is that why you really work for him? Not hungry," I said.

"I work for him because I made a deal. You should eat so you'll get back your strength. And stop acting like a child; this isn't a game."

"What's with King and deals? Is he Monty Hall? Did he brand you, too? I'm not acting like a child, but you two are treating me like one. I'm. Not. Hungry. And can we stop having two conversations?"

"I can see you're going to be trouble. God help King."

"God help me."

Mack chuckled. "I'll be back in a few; I've got to take care of some paperwork at the airport. Do not leave this room, Mia, or you'll feel the wrath of two dangerous men."

Nice. "See ya."

I watched Mack leave the room with a little bounce in his step. He seemed like a happy, content-with-his-life sort of guy without any romance-deterring baggage. He was boyishly handsome and confident. He looked pretty damned tough—physically anyway—and he flew planes. What the hell was he doing messed up in all this and working for King?

King.

I didn't want to feel those butterflies deep in my stomach when I thought about the man, but I couldn't help it. Don't get me wrong. They weren't the swoon breed, but the nervous, angry, froth at the mouth sort of butterflies.

Yes, rabid, crazed, angry butterflies of death and destruction. At least, that's what I told myself. In all honesty, I questioned how any part of me, even a tiny part that only came out when I felt intoxicated, could have any romantic feelings for a man like King. For that to happen, there'd have to be something good inside him, some redeeming quality that I felt attracted to.

Maybe there's just something wrong with you.

I slid lethargically from the bed and wandered to the window for another look at the arch. It was evening now, and the sun was just setting. London was actually a lovely city. Why had I never noticed? I'd been there about ten times, but always for business. Airport. Hotel. Office. Restaurant. Hotel. Office. Airport. That was my usual itinerary. I'd never stopped to see Big Ben, Buckingham Palace, or the Natural History Museum. Come to think of it, I was the most traveled person I knew, yet I'd never been anywhere worth talking about or remembering with a photo. I'd been too focused on work and climbing the ladder.

What a waste. I shook my head, trying not to think about what happened in Mexico or how short life was. Those poor, poor men. Who would want to end their lives?

"Feeling better, I see?"

I swiveled to find King standing in all his usual, seductive-and-imposing glory. He wore a thin, black sweater and tailored black pants that hugged every powerful muscle. His hair was neatly combed back behind his ears, and his ashen eyes glimmered from the black frames of his lashes.

I sighed and looked back out the window. "You're like a goddamned ghost, King. And don't you know how to knock?"

"Knocking is for people with manners," he replied. "I don't have time for pretenses."

"Nice," I grumbled.

"'Nice' is also a fucking waste of time, as is your childish pouting. We have a missing person and an artifact to find."

Childish pouting? I shot him a look. "You did something to me, King. You made me sick. You made me see..." I couldn't say it. Just like I couldn't say that I'd asked him to kiss me, and I seemed to remember liking it when he had. I hoped to hell he never brought it up again.

"See the dead?" He gestured toward the sitting area in the corner. "Let us discuss that."

"Yeah, let's." I walked over to the armchair next to the glass coffee table and sat. King took the couch across from me and stretched his thick arms over the back. I got another tiny glimpse of that tattoo on his forearm. I wondered if it was the letter "K." He seemed like the sort of narcissist that might do something like that—tattoo his own initial on his arm. Ode to wonderful me.

Oh, God. Why had I said I liked him? Why? And why had his touch triggered such potent, carnal urges in me?

"So?" I waited.

He grinned and stared at me.

"Why are you looking at me like that?" I asked.

"You surprise me, Miss Turner. That is all."

"Meaning?"

He leaned forward. "Do you truly believe I have the ability to make a person see ghosts? Do I look like," he leaned in a little closer and drilled me with his eyes. I felt that funny feeling deep inside that made my stomach lurch, "God? That I can perform miracles?"

When he put it that way... "No, I guess not. Your point?"

"My point is," he leaned back again, "I have a talent for seeing people for who they are. You, Mia, already possessed the ability to sense and see the residues left behind by people or anything with a powerful energy force. I simply helped unlock who you already were: a person with a sixth sense, a Seer of Light."

Was this why King wanted to own me? He thought I could "see" stuff? *Crazy.*

"Yes, and I *saw* Brian. But he wasn't a ghost. He was alive and speaking to me. I didn't imagine it."

"What you saw were Brian's remnants. Of his soul, so to speak."

"Uh-uh. I spoke to him. We had a conversation," I argued.

"Your brain created a fantasy, a story to explain what it couldn't reconcile against your *perception* of reality. But you did not speak to Brian; he was already dead, and the dead cannot speak, now can they, Miss Turner?"

This was beyond insane. My head began to spin again. I wanted to retch. I leaned forward and covered my face.

"The dizzy sensation will go away once you stop fighting it," he said.

"How is this possible?" I mumbled.

"Once again, I am not God, Miss Turner. I cannot explain why or how. Nor do I waste my time arguing with the facts. I accept them and plan my game accordingly. As must you."

"You're delusional if you think something like this can happen to a person and they'd just accept it without question."

"It's merely a question of priorities, Miss Turner. You can spend your time trying to figure out why you were born this way and understanding the evolutionary science behind it, or you can spend your time looking for your brother. One of the choices is time bound. One is not."

He had a point. "Can you tell me anything? How many there are like me? Is it hereditary?"

He shook his head. "I do not know the details apart from your gift being rare. Extremely rare. But once this is all over, you have my blessing to waste the rest of your life asking questions and searching for answers. In the meantime, I suggest we get on with our task."

Why would we be looking for Justin in London? My gut told me he wasn't here. There was no reason for him to be.

Because a person you made up in your head told you that he'd just seen Justin in Palenque?

Crap. I didn't know what to believe anymore. But I didn't believe he was in London. I'd already told King that I thought the embassy lady had been lying.

I took a deep breath. "I want you to take me back to Mexico." From there, I'd start trying to piece together what had happened at the dig site. Of course, my brother's poor team and their families had to be dealt with, too. *Those poor, poor men.*

"Just as soon as we're done in London."

London. London? What a waste, being here. "Wait. Did you even call the police, King? Or did you just leave those men's bodies buried there?"

"They're dead. My telling the police won't change that, but it will slow us down. The authorities will want a statement, they'll want to know how you found them, and I will end up having to expend large sums of money to have you released quickly."

Ass. "What about their families? They have to be worried sick!"

King stared me down, and his intense gray eyes said he was growing tired of this conversation. Clearly, he couldn't care less.

"You can't keep me here," I said.

"I can; however, I won't have to. You'll stay on your own. And you'll be showered, dressed, and fed in thirty minutes."

"You're evil *and* delusional, too? So talented. Can you also tap dance?"

Without responding, his commanding male figure rose and headed for the door. "I located the man Justin was working with. He was perhaps the last person to see him, as well. Be in the lobby in thirty minutes." He closed the door behind him, leaving me there in my white robe, frothing with anger. *Bastard.*

There was a loud knock at the door. *Funny. Really fucking funny, King.* Was he trying to show me that he knew how to knock?

I stomped my way over and opened it. "I'm not laughing!"

It was a young woman in a burgundy uniform holding a tray. "Where would you like your sandwich, Miss Turner?"

I held back a growl and directed her to the small sitting area.

As King prognosticated, I was fed, showered, and dressed in my last clean outfit: pink T-shirt and jeans. However, and yes, call me spiteful, I wasn't in the lobby in thirty minutes. I made it a point to show up three minutes late. Yes, just to piss him off. Which I knew he was by the way his square jaw ticked. However, he said nothing and simply nodded. He knew he'd won.

"King." I nodded back.

Anger ticked in King's eyes. He gestured toward the revolving door, where the infamous black SUV awaited us.

"Do you have one in every city?" I asked once outside.

"Yes," he replied and opened the car door for me.

"Good evening, Miss Turner."

Arno? "You got one of those in every city, too, King?" I asked.

King gave me a "don't waste my time" sort of look.

"Hey, Arno. How are you?" I asked.

I slipped in and shivered. The fall night was drizzly and brisk, and I hadn't packed a coat.

King reached behind my seat and handed me a black leather jacket lined with some sort of white fur. I wasn't a fur wearer, but I was freezing and doubted that King would let me stop at the local Wally for a hoodie or a slicker.

"Thanks." I slipped it on and zipped it up. It hugged my chest, waist, and arms like it had been made for my body. A perfect fit. I didn't want to ask where he'd gotten it from or if it had been made for me. Then I'd feel guilty and have to be nice to him. Okay. Never mind. No, I wouldn't. Besides, in his words, being nice was a waste of time.

"So," I said, "are you going to tell me more about this mysterious man we're about to visit?"

King's eyes focused on the road ahead, and I scooted a few inches closer to my door. The way he took up the space in the back seat, his potent, virile vibe, made me feel more than uncomfortable.

"No mystery," he replied. "His name is Vaughn. He is a collector of sorts."

I knew that name, in fact…"That's the name Guzman mentioned at the airport." I'd forgotten about it. Perhaps on purpose. Just like I tried to forget everything about that day.

King didn't seem surprised.

"How do you know him?" I asked. "How did you find out my brother had contact with him?"

"We happen to have a few mutual acquaintances who also happened to overhear Vaughn speaking about your brother's work."

This couldn't be a coincidence. Not possible.

"Does he have something to do with this Artifact you mentioned?" I asked.

King stilled. "Perhaps."

"Why do you want it so badly?"

"I am also a collector of sorts. It is something I've been trying to locate for a very long time."

"This has *what* to do with my brother?" I asked.

"Everything. It has everything to do with your brother."

I was about to ask yet another question, but I'd worn out my question-welcome. King held up his hand to silence me. "Enough, Miss Turner. In fact, I'd appreciate it if you simply didn't speak until after we meet with Vaughn."

Rude. King acted like he was a real king. Maybe the name had gone to his head.

"Why are you bringing me?" I asked.

He growled. "I was getting to that. Perhaps, if you'd cease with the questions, I might be able to explain myself."

I wanted to claw at his horrible, beautiful face. Instead, I picked up a newspaper that had been folded and shoved in the seat pocket in front of me.

He continued. "I want you to look around his office and commit to memory everything you see. Specifically, if you see any residuals of the Artifact.

That, however, is all you are to do. You may leave the questions to me."

I grumbled something unladylike and opened the paper.

"This is serious, Miss Turner. You will remain quiet."

Chances were slim. Whatever terror-induced silence King had been able to subdue me with in the past was no longer effective. Maybe things changed the minute I started talking to dead people and seeing colors. King's scare factor got bumped down a few notches.

I illuminated the overhead light and focused on the paper. It was the only thing I could do to suppress the volcano of angry emotions just begging to bubble out and ooze all over the backseat.

"Miss Turner," King said with a stern slowness, "do you understand?"

I dropped the paper. "Let's cut the crap, okay? If you want me to start 'understanding,' you'll have to tell me the why."

Amusement flickered in King's heavenly eyes, making me nervous. The last time I'd challenged him—about my brother's team being alive and well—and he didn't push back, I ended up having my world tipped upside down. That look in his eyes meant he might simply get out of my way and let me run myself over. It meant I was getting into something I didn't understand.

"What aren't you telling me about Vaughn?" I asked.

At that moment, the rain started coming down in buckets. The SUV filled with the sound of water pelting the windshield, which only upped my anxiety for some reason.

King scratched the thick growth of stubble on his jaw, then glanced at his watch. "He's a psychopath. And when he wants something, he'll move heaven and earth to get it."

"Sounds a little like someone else I know," I mumbled.

King's hand landed on my wrist, and I gasped. "Don't ever," he snarled, "compare me to him, Mia. We are nothing alike."

I waited for more, but King left it at that and released me.

"I'm sorry," I said, feeling completely shocked by King's reaction. What kind of man was Vaughn that King would lose his calm like that? "Can you please explain, though, why you're so worried about me speaking when we meet with him?"

The rain turned to hail, and it sounded like we were being pelted with rocks.

King's magnificent frame grew more rigid. "If you do anything other than stand there pretending to be a cute piece of ass tonight, he might notice you're different."

A shiver of disgust crawled over my skin. "So you're saying he'd try to take me?"

"He would *try*." King's words also meant that Vaughn would fail. At least, that's what I hoped he meant. I didn't want to ask how King, in this very strange, hypothetical situation, would stop Vaughn. I might not like the answer.

Instead, I asked, "So you really think I'm a Seer?"

"Of Light. Yes, I do." King looked ahead, frowning a bit. "If you still need convincing, this is your chance."

The SUV pulled to the side of the street. "We're here, sir," Arno said.

"Where's here?" I asked, taking note of the graffiti on the buildings and crumpled wads of wet garbage on the sidewalk.

"Brixton," King replied.

Again, I didn't know London well, but I gathered that this was not the nice part. "Is it safe?"

King laughed. "For me, yes. For you, only when you're with me."

Arno walked around to the passenger side with a giant black umbrella and opened the door. I stepped out onto the flooding sidewalk. And in that one fraction of a second, right before Arno shut the door, I caught a glimpse of the back of that newspaper I'd been holding in my hand. Federale *Shot at Mexico City Airport After Torturing and Killing Four Co-Workers.*

My knees nearly buckled, but Arno caught my arm and steadied me. "Miss Turner? Are you all right?"

He probably thought it was just another of those dizzy spells.

"Uh, yeah." I nodded agitatedly, trying to hide my panic attack. Was that King's doing?

Oh my god. Who else? It was more than a coincidence that there had been four other people that day, aside from Agent Guzman, who'd assisted him.

So King was a ruthless killer? To be honest, I didn't feel much sympathy for those thugs. Not after they'd threatened to violate me. What bothered me was that King was the sort of person who would and apparently had murdered people. It took a special breed of person to kill. I was working for him.

Shit. Mack wasn't joking when he'd said that King was dangerous, but what should I have expected? Normal, nice people didn't go around asking other nice people to be their slaves or brand them like cattle.

Normal, nice people didn't go around seeing dead people, either. So what did that make me?

Over my head and scared shitless. But I didn't know what to do. It's not like I could run away. This dodgy part of town would gobble me up in a heartbeat.

Arno hurried me to the overhang of a small convenience store we'd parked in front of. King was already there, holding open the door.

I stopped and looked up at him. "I think I'll wait in the car. I'm not feeling well."

King gripped my wrist, right where he'd tattooed me, and the pressure sent mind-numbing bolts of pain through my system.

"Get inside," he commanded.

Suddenly, I wanted to do just that. *What is happening to me?* But that question faded away along with my resolve to escape.

I stepped inside like an obedient dog. The place was cramped, and the shelves crammed with junk food. The floors were grubby, and the plastic panels covering the overhead lights were cracked or missing. What did Vaughn collect? Dirt?

The clerk jerked his head toward us and went back to whatever he was watching on his phone.

Still holding my wrist, King dragged me toward the back of the store through a set of double doors. It was dark, with boxes and garbage piled against the walls so high it reached the mold-covered ceiling.

At the very back of the room was a door with peeling white paint. King opened it, not bothering to knock. "Vaughn," I heard King say.

I tried to see around King, but he was pretty damned big compared to me.

"King, always a pleasure. And I see you've brought me the girl."

"What?" I miraculously tugged my arm free from King and took a step back but was blocked by several large men holding tire irons. Where had they come from?

They pushed me past King, inside the dank-smelling office with wood-paneled walls and a rotten old couch, which one of the men made me sit on.

"What the hell, King?" I hissed.

"Shut the fuck up," he said to me and then glanced at the scraggly looking man with salt-and-pepper hair in his sixties, wearing a ratty, old brown cardigan, sitting behind the desk, where tall stacks of disheveled papers leaned precariously toward the floor.

"Do you have what I want?" King asked him.

The man instructed his two thugs to wait outside, then jostled his lips from side to side. "I believe I have located it, yes. And now that I see you have the girl, I will proceed in acquiring it."

I couldn't believe this. King was going to barter me away? This must have been his plan all along.

Vaughn made a loud hacking sound and then cleared a ball of sticky phlegm from his throat. "I don't suppose you'd like to leave her here with me?" He planted his elbows on the desk and opened his pruney, pallid hands. His beady eyes and leathery, yellowish skin reminded me of a snake. "As a gesture of goodwill," Vaughn added.

King laughed. "I don't do credit, and I want the Artifact by tomorrow."

Vaughn laughed and then scraped the edges of his mouth. "I need a week."

"Two days," King replied, "or I sell the girl to another bidder."

That's when it clicked. Vaughn was a human trafficker. That's what King had meant by "a collector of sorts."

The room turned into a mess of red lights swirling over the walls, the desk, the floor, and...my eyes floated down, horrified to see the couch bathed in red. Was that because people had been murdered in this place?

Oh my god, you're next. I wanted to vomit. Cold sweat broke out on my brow. I leaned forward and braced myself on the edge of Vaughn's desk.

"She's sick," Vaughn said, as if I were tainted meat.

"She'll be fine. It is just a cold." King glared down at me with those steely eyes. "Isn't that right, Veronica?"

Veronica? He'd lied to Vaughn about my name. Was King trading me away to this decrepit monster of a man or was King playing him? I didn't know.

I looked around the room again. The wood paneling dripped with syrupy red blood that wasn't really there.

Holy crap. I quickly had to choose between trusting King or calling his bluff with an apparent serial killer who wanted me as a sex slave. *I decided against becoming the* Bride of Chucky.

I nodded dumbly and then faked a sneeze. "Just a cold."

Vaughn smiled. "Then I should get a discount. For what it's costing me to acquire your stupid little trinket, I could buy five just like her."

"But they won't have that ass, those tits, and they won't be virgins." King gripped my wrist and pulled me up from the couch. "Let's go."

Ass. Tits. Virgin. Were those my selling points? For the record, I was no virgin.

We were just outside Vaughn's office door when his two thugs blocked us. I hadn't really noticed on the way in, but the two brawny-looking dudes with flabby arms and thick bellies were more mass than brawn.

"Move," King commanded, his voice pure menace.

I know it sounds strange, but I understood that death was a part of life, and I'd gladly take someone down with my own two hands if it meant saving myself from being murdered or raped. Short of that, I didn't want to watch anyone die. Yet, as the tattoo on my arm began to tingle, I knew I was about to see it happen anyway.

"Vaughn," King said, his eyes sharply pinned to one of the men, "are you sure you want this? Because I'm not leaving without the girl, and you'll have one hell of a mess to clean up."

Vaughn hadn't moved from his desk. "I have another proposal. You leave the girl, and we let you walk with only one of your arms missing."

King quickly glanced at me. "Close your eyes."

I didn't want to, but like before, I couldn't stop myself from obeying him. My lids reluctantly slid over my pupils. The door to Vaughn's office slammed shut, leaving him inside, I presumed, and leaving us in the dark, disgusting storeroom alone with Vaughn's two thugs. I didn't hear screams or any sounds of a struggle. I simply heard a whoosh of air and then two sad little gurgles.

"Let's go." King's powerful grip tugged me out of my stupor. I opened my eyes, stumbled forward, and flashed a glance over my shoulder. The two men lay face down in a pool of blood.

Ohmygod. Ohmygod. He killed them. He killed them. Don't panic, Mia. Stay calm.

When we got inside the SUV, Arno calmly drove away like we'd just made a stop for a refreshing Fresca and a bag of Doritos. I didn't dare say a word. Don't get me wrong. There was a cataclysmic fear hammering away inside my chest over what just happened, but now I knew without a doubt that I had to get away from King. He'd killed those men in less than a second, he'd done something to my mind, and I was sure he'd killed those officials at the Mexico City airport. King was dangerous, perhaps even more than that psycho back at the store.

Who had I gotten myself mixed up with?

Fuck. I had to get away. Every step I took only pulled me deeper and deeper into a situation I wasn't equipped to handle or comprehend.

I bit my tongue and focused on my breath. My passport and things were back at the hotel. I would grab them, take a cab to the airport, and get the first flight to anywhere.

I am so sorry, Justin. I hope you're okay. After all, I'd done all this for him, but only to tragically get myself tangled up in some horrible mess.

"I'm surprised, Miss Turner," said King.

"Oh?" I kept my focus on the nocturnal scenery—rows and rows of houses butted right up against each other and covered with graffiti.

"No questions? No snide remarks?" he said.

"Not really. You did what you had to," I said, playing it cool. I began to hum "A Hard Day's

Night" by the Beatles, but then stopped myself. Humming wasn't going to soothe away this much anxiety.

"I always protect what's mine," he said with a venomous scowl. "And did you do what I asked?"

"Mine." It felt so strange to hear him refer to me as his possession. It created an unusual little tingle right where my heart was.

"I didn't see anything," I lied.

"I find that rather odd."

"It doesn't matter what you think. I didn't see anything," I lied again. Maybe if he thought I was of no use to him, he'd let me go. "Maybe I'm not this light-seer person you think I am."

"Then why is your heart pounding like you've just seen a horrible monster and you want to flee?"

Hold it in, Mia. Hold it in. "I watched two men die after a botched attempt to sell my body to a mass murderer."

As soon as I said "mass murderer," I knew I'd slipped up. That meant I'd seen something in that office to tell me Vaughn had killed people there.

Oddly, King didn't call me out on my lie. "That was not how I'd planned the event to unravel, and before you interject another of your witty colloquialisms, my plan was not to sell you. My only objective was to get you inside long enough to look around. I did not anticipate that Vaughn would want you so badly."

Insult or compliment? I wasn't sure.

"Then why not tell me your plan going in?" I asked.

"You are no actress, Miss Turner. I did what was needed to sell the story."

"Which was?"

King looked away and stared out the window. "I told him you were someone else. It doesn't matter now."

I scoffed. "And what did you ask in return? For that stupid Artifact? What is it, anyway? A bowl or a cup for your Inca collection?" After all, I suspected that's really what this had become about. King could care less about finding my brother unless it was a means to his precious little Artifact.

"The Artifact isn't Incan. Nor is it pre-Hispanic. But none of that matters because Vaughn lied. Vaughn doesn't have it, or he would have traded for you right there on the spot."

Great. "And what's to stop him from coming after me?"

"He doesn't know who you are, and I wouldn't worry about it now even if he did," King replied.

That was a strange response because I sure as hell was worried. "Why?"

King's beautiful eyes glittered in the dark. "He won't come after you because now he'll have his sights set on something infinitely more valuable."

"What? The Artifact?"

"No. Me."

I laughed. That was the funniest damned thing I'd heard all day. "He wants to make you his sex slave? That's scary."

King leaned back in the black leather seat and allowed his superbly masculine body to take up most of the space: long legs stretching toward my feet, one large arm extending over the backseat, touching my shoulder. "That certainly would be frightening, but no."

I tried to inch away, but I was practically against the door as it was. "So why would Vaughn want you?"

"As I said, he is a collector of sorts."

He collects arrogant, rich bastards?

King mumbled something to himself and pushed up his left sleeve. The orange streetlamps flickered across the interior of the vehicle, and I caught a glimpse of his forearm. Contrary to my earlier guess, his tattoo wasn't like mine. King's was a sundial about four inches wide and the most intricate body art I'd ever seen. The effects were astonishing, as if the dial stood up like a shark fin from his skin. And the roman numerals were raised, too, giving the design a sort of lifelike movement to it.

"When we return to the hotel," King noticed my eyes fixated on his arm and pushed down his sleeve, "you will stay with Mack while I take care of a few things."

I wondered if King meant he was going to "take care" of Vaughn just like he'd taken care of those people at the airport. Didn't matter. I was getting the hell out of there.

"Sure. Whatever," I responded.

King's pupils suddenly looked like those of an animal when caught in the headlights.

I held in a gasp.

"Do not think of going anywhere on your own, Miss Turner. It is not safe out there for you."

Clearly. And it wasn't safe with King, either. Yes, he'd kept me from being taken, but that didn't mean he wasn't dangerous.

The SUV pulled up to the hotel.

"Stay with Mack," King said. "This is not a request."

I nodded, opened the door, and entered the lobby. Feeling his eyes watching my every step, I tried to keep the pace of my stride calm and collected; I didn't want King to sense the horrible panic undulating just beneath the surface.

As soon as I was out of sight, I rushed to my room, grabbed my passport from the safe in the closet, and went into the bathroom to get my toothbrush. When I came out, I unexpectedly saw Mack on the bed, eating some snack from the mini-bar, drinking a beer, and watching rugby on TV.

I yelped.

"Hey, I ordered a sandwich for you. Wanna watch the game?" He muted the channel.

"I'm not hungry. Where the hell did you come from?

He shot me a glance. "The room next door."

"Knocking would be really nice next time."

He looked at the stuff in my hands. "Where do you think you're going?"

"I thought I'd go to the gym for a few minutes. I need to work off some serious anxiety."

He took a sip of beer, but kept his eyes on the match. "Yeah. I just heard. Sorry I missed the fun."

"How did you hear?"

"King called right after he dropped you off. He said the meeting didn't go well."

"Did he tell you he killed two guys?"

Mack shrugged. "I'm sure they had it coming."

That was his response?

"And, no," he added, "you can't go to the gym. You're staying here."

I glowered. "Are you prepared to physically keep me from leaving this room?"

Mack sighed, dusted off his hands, and swung his legs to the floor. "Mia, don't do this. You're a smart young woman, and I am an extremely well-trained man. If I wasn't, why would King trust your safety to me?"

"I just want to go to the gym, Mack."

"If you really want to work off some stress, there are other ways."

His statement was not accompanied by a suggestive smirk or an innocent example such as yoga or meditation, so I wasn't sure what he'd meant. Therefore, I opted to respond with a frown—a safe bet, just in case he was testing the hookup waters.

"You're not leaving." He stood from the bed and towered over me. When Mack wasn't serious, his face had a playful, boyish look to it—lively blue eyes, messy blond hair, and a funny smile. He reminded me a little of Justin. But when this man was serious, I could see he went to the King school of intimidation. His "don't fuck with me" gaze was well rehearsed as was his menacing body language.

I threw up my hands. "Fine, Mack. You win. I'll stay. But then you have to swing by the gift shop and buy my tampons."

His Adam's apple bobbed with a swallow.

"And some pads," I added. "I sleep with pads. Extra thick so I don't leak. My flow is really heavy on the first day."

Again he swallowed. I could smell the fear.

Bad ass, my ass.

"I'll go with you and stand outside while you buy them," he muttered.

"Wimp." I threw everything on the bed, except for my passport and wallet, and headed out the door.

He didn't argue, and I could swear that during the entire elevator ride down to the lobby, the man's face sizzled red.

Seriously? The period thing was the oldest trick in the book.

Well, lucky me, I supposed.

We walked to the small convenience store at the back of the lobby, where Mack stood outside the window watching me like a hawk as I perused the array of sundries. *Crap.* I needed him to look away for a minute. Just one lousy minute. Didn't matter which way, either. I could slip out the back or the front. Instead, those puppy-dog eyes, filled with reserved caution, watched closely. I had to do something.

I grabbed the biggest box of tampons and held them up. "Hey, Mack!" I shook the box high in the air, causing the other two customers, the clerk, and a few lucky guests passing by the entrance to look at me. "I don't know these brands. Which do you think is better for the gusher between my legs? I don't want to stain the sheets. It's such a nice hotel!"

Mack frowned and blew out an uncomfortable breath, cheeks inflated and everything. He turned away, pretending he didn't know me.

"Mack! Hey, Mack!" I yelled.

He crossed his arms, stared at his feet, and sort of slinked away. He was just a few yards from the entrance, but it was all I needed.

I dropped the box, bolted out the door, and headed to the back exit of the hotel. One and a half blocks away, I grabbed a taxi.

"Heathrow," I told the driver, but then realized that would be the first place Mack and King would look. I couldn't get on a plane. Not yet, anyway.

But you can get on a train.

"Excuse me, ma'am?" I said to the driver. "Can you take me to the train station instead? Not the closest one. Make it a few stations away."

She gave me a look, but didn't argue.

"And could we stop by a bank on the way there?"

I'd have to withdraw some cash and keep moving every time I did that. Otherwise, they'd be able to track me down. I felt my phone vibrate in my leather jacket.

Crap. It was probably Mack or King asking where the hell I'd gone. I'd have to turn it off.

I dug it from my pocket and looked at the screen. "Oh my God, Justin."

"Mia, I told you not to come looking." Justin sounded furious, but I couldn't care less.

"Goddammit. Where are you, Justin? *Where?*"

There was a pause. "You need to go home, Mia. Tell Mom and Dad that I love them, but not to come looking, either."

"No. Goddammit. What's wrong with you? Are you mixed up with that Vaughn man? He's dangerous, Justin! Do you hear me? He's a killer. He buys women and kills them."

"Mia, what the fuck did you do?" He laughed with a bitter groan. "Shit. I can't believe this."

"Justin, what. Is. Going. On?"

"Mia. You have absolutely no idea what you're getting mixed up in. Don't go near Vaughn. Just go home. You can't help me."

"Come with me. Are you here in London?"

"Fuck. You're in London? Get the hell out of there! They'll use you to get to me. They'll kill you."

"Who's they?" I asked. "King? Is King one of them?"

"I don't know King, but you can't trust anyone. They have eyes everywhere. And stay the fuck away from Vaughn."

Had he lost his mind? And who was "they"?

"Justin, did he kill your team? Does this have to do with that Artifact?"

There was another long pause. "Mia, I won't be calling you anymore. I can't risk it. Just…Mia, go home. Tell Mom and Dad I'm sorry. That I didn't know what I was doing. I love you."

The call ended, and I simply stared at the empty screen. The breath slipped from my lungs, and the life drained from my body. I felt myself being washed away, carried off in the current of this nightmare. The tears trickled from my eyes. "I can't go home, Justin," I whispered. I was now stuck in this mess, too.

CHAPTER TEN

When I arrived at the Edinburgh station, it was just before midnight, and I immediately asked around for the nearest hotel-slash-motel-slash-whateverwithabed. I needed to close my eyes somewhere safe and think things through. The long train ride had done little more than give me another migraine and heighten my sense of dread. Was it because I knew that running from King wasn't a permanent solution? Sooner or later, that man would find me. After all, he could find anything or anyone. Except the Artifact and my brother, apparently.

Shit. My brother... What was I going to do about my parents? It wasn't like Justin to be out of touch for so long, and the lie I'd told them had expired. I should be back at home by now from my fake trip. With me nowhere to be found, they'd be panicking. They'd be shattered. But what the hell could I tell them? The truth was out of the question, they wouldn't believe another lie, and if I tried to feed them the bullshit that Justin fed me, then they'd do exactly what I had: come looking.

"What a shitty situation." I trudged my way up the stairs to the third floor of the small hotel. The building was old and smelled like an antique shop. I had no clue why I chose this city of all places, but I simply wanted to get out of London, and Edinburgh was the next train to depart.

I supposed, too, that King wouldn't look for me here. Once he figured out that I hadn't gotten on any flights, which I was sure he would, then he'd start checking places he'd know were familiar to me and, perhaps, traveled to previously for work. How would he know that? That man probably knew everything about me, including my bra size. He'd known about Sean—the guy in New York I "dated" casually. No one knew about him. Not even Becca. King also knew that I hummed Beatles songs when I got nervous and that my favorite "stress-elixir" was whiskey.

I unlocked the hotel door, flipped on the lights, and sighed. It was a gloomy, cramped room with brown carpet and a small bed. Still, it was better than nothing.

I locked the door behind me, flipped off the lights, and lay down, covering my eyes with my forearm. Tomorrow, when my head cleared, I'd think out options.

"Hello, Miss Turner."

I bolted to an upright sitting position. The tall, imposing shadow of King's frame lurking in the corner was unmistakable.

I blinked several times. "Impossible," I whispered. This had to be another one of those crazy dreams.

King stepped toward the bed, the lights from the street illuminating his face. His beautiful, luminescent eyes burned with the kind of fury that could stop a person's heart. "No. Not impossible."

"But how?"

He grabbed my wrist and yanked me up from the bed as if I were no lighter than a feather pillow. "Have you forgotten?" His hard body pressed against mine as he towered over me, his iron grip threatening to crush my bones. He turned my wrist over, shoving his brand in my face. "I own you, Mia. You cannot run from me, but you can be killed."

"Is-is that why you're here? T-to kill me?" Because I feared for my life. I truly did. How the hell had he found me?

A sinister smile crept over his gorgeous mouth. "You're of no use to me dead. But I do plan to punish you." He released my wrist and forcefully cupped the back of my head. When his lips smashed into mine, his mouth was hot, his kiss rough. My knees buckled. He wrapped his arm around my back and pinned me to him. I wanted to pull away, but the friction of his stubble, the silky heat of his tongue invading my mouth, and the hardness of his male body subdued me. Or was it this strange power he held over me? I didn't know. I just wanted more. My nipples contracted into sharp little points, and a throbbing ache deep inside urged me to lean deeper into his hips, to seek the hard flesh I knew was there, to find that release of tension he triggered inside me.

What was happening to me? Why couldn't I stop myself from thinking that if I was his, then he was mine? Mine to use. Mine to take from. Mine to ravage and savor and claw at if it pleased me.

"You want me, King?" I growled. "Then I hope you can fuck like a beast."

King's large hands slid down the small of my back and gripped my ass. He ground himself against me and released a deep, throaty groan. "I'm going to break you, Mia. Fucking break you."

My eyes popped open, and I gasped, finding nothing but an empty, dark hotel room. "Crap." *Not again.*

I held my hand over my heart, hoping that it might stop the pounding. But it didn't. I ran my hand over my hair and felt the sticky sweat covering my skin—forehead, neck, and chest. I couldn't run from him, could I? He was in my head. My body was saturated with him or his energy or...*crap*...*something*. I didn't know. I realized that the repeated dreams weren't simply random fears trying to escape my subconscious. They were a glimpse into some twisted part of my soul that felt connected to this man. But that part of me could never see the light of day. Never. Because wanting King was like wanting to have a heroin addiction. It was like wanting to die a slow, painful death.

Still sitting on the bed, I hung my head. "What am I going to do?" I mumbled.

"You are going to get the fuck up from that fucking bed before I tie you up and ship you off in a box to Vaughn."

I gasped. "King?"

"In the fucking flesh, woman."

King flipped on the lights, and I leaped from the bed, trying to put any sort of distance I could between us. His face looked different somehow, as if it was an angrier, more lethal version of him. But he wore his crisp, tailored, black suit. He smelled like King's expensive cologne. That scowl on his face was certainly his. Yet, it wasn't King. An imposter. Because there was no physical way King could be there with me.

"Who are you?"

King tilted his head to one side. "Who the fuck do you think I am?"

"You're not King. You can't be. I left King back in London."

"Mia, I don't have time for this bullshit."

"I'm Mia, now?" I grabbed the phone from the nightstand and raised the hand piece into the air. "Stay away from me."

"Are you planning to call my mother?" he seethed.

I wasn't laughing. Then again, neither was he.

"I'm not leaving with you, whoever you are," I said.

He crossed those familiar, thick arms over his chest, making his broad, square shoulders appear even wider than they were. "I *really* don't have time for this."

He sighed.

I blinked.

He was somehow on me, grabbing my arm.

I screamed. How had he gotten over to me so quickly?

He flipped my wrist and placed his palm over my tattoo. "Shut up."

I snapped my lips shut and stared at him, wondering how he'd managed to control me like this again.

"We're leaving." He tugged me out the door, into the hall, and down the stairs. I wanted to yell at him. I wanted to say that he couldn't do this to me, but my mind and body were not one.

As we walked past the reception area, the woman at the desk asked if I was all right. But I just kept on walking, King dragging me behind him like an insolent child.

The night air was frigid and cold, causing a sheen of mist to immediately coat my face. When we reached the street corner, King held up my hand to flag a passing taxi. It stopped, and King pushed me inside. I wondered where Arno was.

"Tell the driver we are going to Prestonfield House," King said. Why didn't he just tell the man himself? Because King was trying to prove a point while scaring the crap out of me. He wanted to demonstrate his absolute power over me. But he didn't have to; I knew. Fucking hell, I knew.

"Now!" King barked.

What the driver must think of me, letting some horrible man speak to me that way. I cleared my throat. "Ummm. Prestonfield House, please."

The driver nodded, but didn't turn around. I was glad not to have to face him. And it wasn't as if he could help me.

My body began to tremble violently, and I felt that familiar wave of toxic nausea saturate my innards.

I started to pant through my nose.

King released my wrist, and I immediately felt better. *Holy shit. What is going on?*

I stole a glance at King, but when I saw how he stared at me, a feral, dark gaze like he wanted to rip my head off, I looked away.

"Why are we going to Prestonfield House?" I asked.

"It's nah where ya wanted teh go?" The driver looked at me through the rearview mirror.

"Oh. Sorry. I was talking to him." I gestured toward King.

The driver furrowed his brows and kept driving.

Several minutes of awkward silence passed without a peep from my mysterious captor.

"So?" I asked.

I don't know what sort of answer I expected from King. After all, he'd just hunted me down in an obscure hotel room, possessed me with some sort of strange mind-control crap yet again, and now...

The taxi pulled up to an impressively large, historic-looking building with neoclassic columns at the entrance. Bright white lights bathed the front of the plastered structure, making it difficult to see. Regardless, the well-dressed Scotsman in a dark kilt who greeted me immediately signaled that this was yet another posh hotel.

"Pay the man," said King.

"You have got to be kidding," I hissed, but it wasn't because King had asked me to pay the cab; it was because he'd made me come to this place. Whatever King had to say or do could've been done back at the crappy motel. Or did it offend his delicate senses to torture me in such a dump?

"Thank you very much," I said and handed the driver a bill.

I slipped out and told the bellhop that I didn't have any luggage. He gave me a quick look and welcomed me anyway.

"Tell the receptionist you want my usual suite," said King.

Usual suite? "This is crazy. You're craz—" King grabbed my wrist. "Do it, Mia. Or I will make you."

I didn't want him to do that thing to me again; it was horrible and frightening not to be in charge of your own body.

I didn't say a word and just went inside. My first impression was that we'd entered a seventeenth-century museum. The long, narrow corridor leading to the lobby had deep purple walls, pillars on each side, and plush, velvety curtains with matching upholstered chairs positioned every ten or so feet.

"Why are we here, King?"

"Just walk," he ordered.

About halfway down the corridor, he said, "Tell them you work for King Enterprises and that you're in town on a last minute buying trip."

"But I—"

"If you ask me one more question, Miss Turner, it will be your fucking last. I swear it."

I sucked back the burst of contempt my ego felt from the slap because I had no doubt that King would hurt me. "Fine. Okay."

I approached reception and glanced up at the clock. It was one in the morning, so I had to ring the bell. A sleepy-eyed, young brunette immediately greeted me.

"Hi. I know it's late, but I'm here on a last minute buying trip for King Enterprises. Would you happen to have a room?"

She yawned. "Of course, Miss…?"

"Miss Turner."

She typed away on her computer. "Ah, yes, ma'am. There ye are. How many nights will ye be stayin'?"

I couldn't believe this. She had me in her system?

"Uhhh…" I looked at King.

"Two. Maybe three," he growled.

I turned and looked at the lady, but she simply stared, then repeated the question.

"Like he said, two, maybe three," I said.

She lifted her brows and returned to her screen. "We have Mr. King's usual suite."

How could King have a usual anything in Edinburgh?

She made a few more strokes on her keyboard and handed me a key. "Should I call for the—"

"No. No luggage. Thank you," I said.

She gave me a quick nod. "Enjoy your stay, Miss Turner. If ya be needin' anything, please give us a ring."

"Thanks." I flashed a nervous smile and then followed King to the elevator.

Once we were inside with the door closed, King had me by the lapel of my leather jacket. He lifted me against the wall. "If I lose the Artifact because of you, I swear I'll kill your brother myself and make you watch."

I struggled against him, but his grip was as solid as the rest of him.

"Why don't you just kill me, instead? I know you want to, so get it over with. I sure as hell prefer that over being your lapdog, King."

He took a breath and released me, mumbling in a foreign language I didn't recognize. He straightened his black silk tie, and the doors slid open. I didn't want to go with him. I was certain he wanted to hurt me.

When King noticed I hadn't exited the elevator, he reached inside and pulled me out by the hand. I stumbled and barely kept from falling. He dragged me down another hallway with a decorum similar to the lobby's rich, dark colors—deep reds, purples, and chocolate browns. Silk tapestries, lavish antique armchairs, beveled mirrors, and oil paintings of long-gone aristocrats from the days of lace and velvet gave the entire place the feel of having walked back in time.

We entered the suite, and it was no different. King closed the door after me, and I stood in the entry, cautiously watching him walk to the table next to the large bed. He opened a bottle of scotch, poured a tall glass, and held it out for me.

I didn't move. I couldn't move.

"Take it, Mia. You'll need it. Trust me."

Without removing my eyes from the man, I walked over and took the glass.

"Sit." He pointed to the plush eggplant-colored couch behind me.

"I don't want to sit."

"Sit!" he barked.

I glared at him. "How long are you planning to do this?"

"What? You're not enjoying the way I treat you?"

I took a sip of the scotch and savored its smoky sweetness. Well, if I was going to die, at least I'd go out with one good memory.

"Not particularly," I said.

He bobbed his head and then removed his coat, leaving on his starched white shirt and black silk tie. "I should kill you for disobeying me, Mia." He laid his coat on the bed and loosened his tie, his piercing gray eyes watching me intently. "But I still need you. So I think a punishment is in order." He tossed the tie onto the bed and unbuttoned the top of his shirt.

My hand began to tremble violently, remembering the dream I'd had when he'd said he wanted to break me.

I swallowed, set my glass down on the small table beside the couch, and sat. My mind suddenly flooded with the images from my dream. I looked down at my feet, my head spinning. What was I going to do? This wasn't a dream, and I didn't want him to touch me.

"Mia, what do you suggest?" He sat on the edge of the bed, legs open, hands laced together as he leaned in, elbows perched on his thighs in a stately way.

I didn't respond.

"Look at me when I speak to you," he snarled.

I ignored his command, but it took every ounce of willpower I had. "How did you find me?"

"I used the mark on your wrist."

My head snapped up. *Holy shit.* We really were connected? But how could a tattoo do that? "You're a witch, aren't you?"

He frowned. "I believe the correct term is warlock, but no. Warlocks are fictional."

"Then what are you? A demon? A creature from another world?"

King laughed into the air, and it was a beautiful laugh. Beautiful and wicked, just like the man. "I think you read too many silly books, Mia." He stood, walked over to the table, and poured himself a drink, giving me his back. "I'm sorry to disappoint you, Miss Turner, but there are only two types of people in this world: living or dead. I'm afraid there isn't much in between."

"But you just said you found me using this." I pointed to my wrist.

He turned and raised his glass to me. "That I did."

"Then *what* are you?"

"I am a man who acquires things I find useful: people, rare artifacts, wealth, and," he paused and took a sip, "seemingly impossible abilities that allow me to get what I want."

I took that as code for some sort of voodoo. I didn't believe in such things, but when you run out of obvious, rational answers, your mind starts to make leaps. "You mean you put a spell on me?"

The corner of his seductive mouth curled. "Spells are for children's fairytales. I acquire power, or more accurately stated, I obtain ways to channel it and use it to my advantage."

I reached for my glass and took a sip. A really, really big sip. Okay, it was a gulp.

"Don't look so shocked, Miss Turner. You of all people—a Seer of Light—should understand that there are forces in this world beyond our comprehension. It's perfectly plausible that someone with a great amount of determination could learn to harness these forces, just as I've harnessed you and your special abilities."

Was that how he saw what he was doing to me? I was like the sun or the wind? Or perhaps he saw me more like a beast of burden in need of a yoke and a master.

"Is that why you want this Artifact?" I asked. "Does it do something special?"

A bit of joy flickered in his ash-colored eyes. "I do, in fact, want the Artifact for this reason."

"What does it do?"

"This is no concern of yours."

"It is if you're using me and my brother to find it."

"Your only task is to lead me to it, Mia. That's why you were brought to me. That is why you still live and breathe even though you've defied me."

"What do you mean, 'brought to you'?"

"You don't think our meeting was a coincidence, do you?"

"My brother went missing; I came looking for you," I argued.

"True; however, I am the destined owner of the Artifact. It was fate that brought you to me. You were the crumb it wanted me to follow."

Although his words sounded like that of a madman, I now fully understood why King thought of me as his property. And it was why he'd felt he had the right to dictate every aspect of my life. It was why he felt he had the right to do that mind-control thing and tattoo my body.

But he didn't own me. I was not King's, and I never would be.

I stared down at the black "K" on my wrist, trying to figure out some possible way to end this. It was no longer just about finding Justin, but about saving myself, too. It was also about saving my family.

"You can feel it, can you not, Miss Turner? The mark on your wrist tingling when I speak the truth."

I did feel a slight prickly sensation, but I had no idea what it meant. "No, I don't. I only feel the need to have it removed."

"The tattoo?"

I nodded.

"Why would you want that?"

I glared at him.

He ran his hand over his perfectly combed, black hair, messing it up. "I got lucky that day, you know."

"What day?"

"That day in Mexico City. I got lucky. Mack and I were already there, wrapping up a little acquisition. When you didn't show up for your connecting flight, I had Mack ask around while I made some calls. He happened to hear two passengers talking about a young American woman who'd been pulled out of line."

I felt my blood pressure drop. If King had arrived just a few minutes later, my life would have been drastically different at this moment. I suddenly realized I'd never thanked King for that night, and part of me still wanted to, even though I knew that wasn't the reason he was telling me this story. He was trying to explain why he'd marked me. It was all about protecting me—his property—in his eyes.

I sighed. "And then you killed them?"

He grinned. "No. Guzman killed his people. Of course, the suggestion came from me."

"Was it a suggestion he couldn't ignore?" If King could control me, then why not others?

He took a sip from his glass. His lips were shiny and wet with scotch. I tried not to look, but a part of me, the dark part, still wanted what I'd felt and enjoyed in that dream. Hard, hot, sinful…

King stared back, keenly aware of how his mouth had captivated my attention. His own lips twitched like they had an itch he wanted to scratch. "Yes, Miss Turner." King's voice was quiet and gravelly.

I snapped out of it and went back to looking at his jewel-like eyes. Not sure it helped much. "Huh?"

He smiled, and it was that charming, devilish smile. "I said, 'yes.' The suggestion was one that Guzman couldn't ignore."

"How did you even know him?"

He shrugged. "A man with my particular interests in the rare and unusual must have a vast network of eyes always on the lookout. You'd be surprised what turns up in airports." He sipped his scotch. "But Guzman was a vermin and untrustworthy. He deserved to die."

"Oh." I nodded slowly and polished off my drink. So those people had been murdered because of me. I didn't know what to think other than I'd expected to feel a twinge of remorse but didn't. Did that make me coldhearted and vengeful?

"You are not the first person, Miss Turner, who he laid his hands on. But you now bear the distinction of being the last."

I contemplated his words, the facts he'd shared, and tried to believe the unbelievable. Still, it all felt like a bad, bad dream, and at any moment, I'd wake up. Justin would be calling me from Mexico, laughing as he told me about another button he'd found.

"So, are you ready?" King asked.

His imposing form rose from the edge of the bed, and he unbuttoned his shirt a little further.

"Ready for what?" I asked.

His head dipped and speared me with those predatory eyes. "Your punishment."

My pulse immediately raced. "You're joking, right?"

He began rolling up his left sleeve. "You might want to start humming one of those Beatles' songs you like so much."

"What are you doing?" My eyes searched for any sign he was joking.

He took a step closer, and I glanced at that strange tattoo on his forearm. "I'm going to give you a choice, Miss Turner. Pain or pleasure. Of course, the pleasure will be all mine."

Huh? I leaned as far back as I could on the couch, but I was cornered with nowhere to go. Was he really going to do this? "I-I don't understand."

He took another step. He was so close, he could reach down and snap my neck if he wanted.

"We had a deal, Miss Turner." He rolled up his right sleeve. "I would find your brother, and you would work for me indefinitely. You would obey me. You wouldn't ask questions. So far, you've broken every part of our bargain."

I eyed the glass in my hand. I could smash it in his face and get away. "You didn't find my brother, so we're even."

He lifted his dark silky brows. "He's right here in Edinburgh, as is the Artifact. You led me right to it, just as I suspected you might."

I shook my whirling head. I couldn't see straight. I couldn't think straight. "That can't be right. I got on the train. I didn't know—"

"There are no coincidences in this game, Miss Turner. Now answer my question: pain or pleasure?"

I blinked. Was he really going to make me choose?

I had to act quickly. I jumped up and swung at his face with my glass. He caught my wrist in midair. I dropped the tumbler and shrieked in agony. His palm covered the brand on my wrist.

A sinister expression flickered in his beautiful silver eyes. "Then I will choose for you: pleasure."

He squeezed my wrist and held me against his body. I felt a powerful burst of agonizing pain course through my veins. I felt like I was being cut and shredded from the inside out. I wanted to scream, but I couldn't move my mouth or form a sound.

King whispered in my ear, "This is only a taste of me."

It was then that I realized his question had been a trick. I was getting pain either way, and King would enjoy every bit of it.

"Bastard," I managed to eke out before the room turned dark.

The next morning, I stretched my sore body in the soft silky sheets and groaned. Everything touching my skin felt so soothing, so warm, so luxurious.

"Mmmm…" I moaned and flipped onto my stomach. I smiled as the smell of warm bread and fresh coffee filled my nose. I yawned and stretched out my arms to enjoy the texture of the cool sheets at my side, but instead, I found warmth. My fingertips probed and slid. Smooth, firm skin greeted my touch.

Huh? I flattened my palm and reached a little further. I found a round pectoral muscle and soft little pebble of a man's nipple.

"Shit!" I flipped over and sat up. King was lying next to me with his eyes closed, his plump, gorgeous lips relaxed. Dark lashes fanned across his upper cheeks, and his black stubble was a little thicker than usual. The white sheet was gathered around his nether region, but his chest, stomach, and lower abdomen were fully exposed.

What is he doing in bed with me? Naked, no less? As I thought this, my eyes were instantly drawn to the elaborate, black tribal tattoo that started at his collarbone and covered half of his pectoral muscles. It reminded me of those large Egyptian collars made of stone and metal beads that fanned around the neck to form a semicircle above one's chest. Toward the center of the design, there was a small square filled with symbols, as though his tattooed necklace had a large pendent. It was beautiful.

My gaze took in the rest of the scenery filled with ripple after ripple of hard, menacing muscles all the way down to where a thin line of black hair, starting just beneath his belly button, disappeared underneath the sheet.

I sighed appreciatively. Physically, the man was an Adonis. Hard and lean. Strong and rough. Even the swells of his biceps and the taper of his neck to his shoulders were perfect.

My gaze fell a bit lower, and I caught something odd in my peripheral vision. Pink, pale skin. Me! *Holy shit! Why am in my underwear?* I scooped up the top of the sheet and covered my bra. The scene was eerily similar to the dream I'd had only a few days ago.

"From the sound of your frantic heartbeat and near-hysterical breathing," King said, in a low, groggy voice with his eyes closed, "you must be awake."

I was horrified. Had I had sex with King? With that…monster? "Why am I almost naked?"

He rolled over and gave me his back. "Because I fucked you like a beast."

What? Those were the words he used in my dream.

"No. Please, please no." I felt the unwanted tears welling in my eyes.

I watched his back inflate and then deflate with a heavy breath. "Don't flatter yourself, Miss Turner," he said calmly. "You're not my type."

"Why the hell are you naked in bed with me? Why am I in my underwear?"

"I removed your clothing and sent them to the wash after you passed out."

Passed out. Passed out? The memories flooded my brain. *The pain. Oh my god, the pain.* He'd filled my entire body with deep, soul-crunching pain. And the look in his eyes, the way he enjoyed holding me as I agonized, unable to scream or cry, was horrific.

"You...*son of a bitch*!" I pounded on his back with my fists. I hit and clawed with every ounce of hatred and anger I had. "I'll fucking kill you!"

King quickly rolled over and caught my arms, pinning me beneath him. "Calm down."

I lifted my head and pressed my nose to his. "Calm down? You tortured me. You...hurt me."

His eyes twitched. "I taught you a lesson. That is all. And if I wanted to really hurt you, your body certainly wouldn't be in such pristine condition this morning."

"The *condition* of my body isn't what I'm talking about. You got inside my head. You...you...got inside..." My words tapered off when I suddenly realized that I had a naked man pinning my almost-naked body against the bed, our lips inches apart. I felt his heart beating against my breasts, the weight of him blanketing my body, the coarse hair between his legs pressing into my bare hip.

As if King had suddenly realized the same, his pale eyes locked onto mine. The fringe of black lashes and his thick black stubble made every elegant, masculine feature of his beautiful face more pronounced.

Then I felt the heat of his body and the flesh between his legs harden and elongate against my intimate juncture.

He stared into my eyes, and time seemed to stop. I didn't know what to do. I was lost in the inexplicably erotic sensations triggered by our bodies touching.

How could I be feeling like this after what he'd just done? It was impossible. *Impossible!* He had to be doing something to my head.

Slowly, perhaps hesitantly, he lowered his mouth to mine. I closed my eyes and felt my mind melt away into a blissful stream of physical sensations. The heat of his lips, the softness of his tongue slipping inside me, the rough maleness of his body.

A soft sigh escaped my lips as his kiss deepened. I opened my mouth further and allowed him to enter me, to stroke me. And each time he slid his tongue against mine, all I could think of was how good he would feel sliding between my thighs, deeper and deeper.

A dream. Another dream, I thought. *Why do I always dream about King? There is no good inside him.* But I wanted there to be. I did. Then these feelings would all make some sort of sense.

King began to push his rigid cock against me, slowly grinding and allowing me to enjoy the feel of our bodies pressing together, igniting. His hand released my wrist and slid down over my neck and shoulder to begin massaging my breast.

We were suddenly caught up in a cataclysmic frenzy of lust, driven by our bodies and not our minds. His hand then traveled from my breast to my hip and stopped behind my knee, where he gave it a little tug to widen my legs for him.

I groaned when the pressure of his cock hit that sensitive spot head-on.

He moved his mouth over my neck and nuzzled the tender area just below my ear. "I think I found a new punishment; the regret you'll feel after we're done."

Punishment. My eyes sprang open. I looked around the room. *Not a dream. Real!*

I slammed my fist into the back of his shoulder. "Get off!"

He lifted his head and looked at me. "I believe that's what I was about to do," he said in that perfect, gentlemanly tone.

"Not with me, you won't." I pushed him away. "Get off me!"

He rolled over and then swung his feet to the floor, his bare back to me. I could see a strange pattern of scars, like crisscrosses over his entire back, as he panted from the exertion.

"Please. D-don't do that again," I stuttered.

He blew out a slow breath and then gave his neck a little crack. Without a word, he rose from the bed and headed for the bathroom. His ass was a work of art, perfectly formed, round hard mounds of muscle. I tried not to look. I tried not to let his raw masculinity affect me. But I'd never seen a man like him before.

"Your clothes will be here in a minute. Get dressed. We leave in ten." He shut the bathroom door, and I took a moment to process. What had he done to me last night? And why, of all things, had he removed my clothes? What a complete SOB.

There was a light knock. I gathered up the bed sheet and wrapped it around my body. I winced as I made my way to answer the door. My entire body felt sore and tender, like I'd overdone it at the gym.

"Yes?" I looked into the hallway, and a young woman held out a bag.

"Yer clothes, Miss Turner."

"Uh. Thanks." I reached for them.

"And Mr. King says yer teh be downstairs in five minutes. The car'll be waitin'."

"Uhhh…" I glanced at the bathroom just a few feet away. I turned back to the woman. "Mr. King?"

She nodded. "Ay. I just saw him headin' down."

"But I-I…" I pointed to the bathroom. "Never mind. Thank you."

I shut the door and stood outside the bathroom. I wanted to hurl. She couldn't be right. I'd just seen

King enter the bathroom. Was I losing my fucking mind?

I raised my hand to knock, but hesitated. What if he was still inside? Then who had she just seen?

"King?" I knocked on the door, but there was no answer. I pushed it open. Empty. The bathroom was empty.

What's happening to me?

CHAPTER ELEVEN

I don't know how I'd managed to dress, wash my face, brush my teeth, and make my way outside the hotel because I didn't remember doing it. My thoughts had been wrapped around King. How had he disappeared like that? And last night, the way he'd gotten inside my head and chewed me up from the inside out, the way he tracked me down using the mark on my arm, and the way he possessed my body with insatiable lust. Who or what was King besides a dangerous enigma? My brain was stuck, trying to answer the question, but I kept landing on the exact same spot: I didn't know.

Was it really possible for ordinary people to acquire extraordinary powers, as King said he had? Was there more to the world than what one simply saw on the surface?

Yes.

I'd seen the proof with my own eyes when I saw Brian, my brother's dead roommate, along with the red swirling light above his grave. The existence of something *else* was real.

So what did that make me? I'd been so horrified and frantic, I hadn't really been given the chance to let the last few days sink into my bones.

I was a Seer of Light. What did that mean?

"Miss Turner, we need to leave."

Huh?

King's voice emanated from a black Mercedes with tinted windows. He was in the driver's seat, waiting.

Damn. I felt like I was in a walking coma.

"What the hell is taking you so long? I've been calling you for an entire minute," he fumed.

I noticed how King looked exceptionally intimidating today in his dark blue suit, royal blue tie, and dark sunglasses.

I slipped into the sleek car and closed the door.

"Where's Arno?" I asked, realizing I'd never seen King drive.

He rubbed his beard. "Taking care of some business for me today."

"Oh." I watched the trees zoom by as King floored it down the wet lane. The drizzle of rain hadn't stopped.

He turned onto the main avenue, unworried about his speed or crashing, weaving effortlessly in and out of traffic.

"Could you slow down?" I whispered. One more ounce of stress might shatter me into a million pieces.

"I'm not slowing down because you have a hangover," he said coldly. "We've already lost too much time because of your impudence."

"Impudence? My impudence? You took off my clothes last night!" I said.

He grumbled a curse. "You threw up all over yourself. Too much scotch. You threw up on me as well while I assisted you in removing your clothes and brushing your teeth. And, unfortunately, as I was in a hurry to get to Edinburgh to find you and didn't have a chance to pack additional clothes, I had to remove mine for cleaning, as well. And before you ask, my cock and balls prefer a more liberated lifestyle, which is why I wore nothing to bed."

Did he mean he liked to go commando?

"Thanks for that extra info."

As for the throwing up, I didn't remember that, but I realized last night was one giant blur. I remembered the pain, though. I would never forget. It felt like being injected with a horrific concoction of every bad emotion a human being could experience—sorrow, loneliness, and despair.

How he'd done it, I didn't know. But I was pretty darn certain I'd be taking some form of revenge on King just as soon as the opportunity arose.

"So where did you go after," I swallowed, "this morning?"

"I grabbed a towel from the bathroom and left. Why?"

I never saw him leave. And hadn't the door been locked from the inside when the maid brought my clothes? Maybe I was mistaken. After all, I'd been in shock.

"I, uhhhh." My head began to swirl again. I winced and pressed the heels of my palms to my temples.

"Miss Turner, I understand that you're not accustomed to all this, that you've led a small, sheltered little life. But you are in my world now. It's not pretty. It's not right. It's survival. And if you really want to save your brother, then you will need to adapt. You will need to accept that reality is simply different than you believed it to be. This will relieve the pain in your head."

I dropped my hands. "So you're saying that I should accept that you'll hurt me if I don't do what you say? You think I should accept that you think you own me? Or that you have the right to get in bed with me in all your commando glory or use my body when your dick gets hard?"

"Yes. Yes. No—that last one was a mistake." He shrugged. "I am male. My dick gets hard. I'm not always choosy as to who helps me relieve the pressure."

I guess that explained why I went from not being his type to being his type: I had a vagina and was at the right place at the right time.

"Classy." I looked out the window at the wet, gray day, trying to ignore the pounding inside my head.

"I see no need to hide behind pretenses," he said. "I am far too old for that."

Prick. Besides, how old was he? Thirty-two? Thirty-five? "So where are we going?"

"As I told you last night, I found Justin. He is here in Edinburgh with the Artifact."

"What? You didn't tell me that last night!" I yelled.

"I promise you, I did. You simply forgot."

I returned to rubbing my temples. "Not possible." I couldn't forget something so important.

He cleared his throat. "Yes, well, perhaps you were a bit preoccupied at the time." A smirk flickered across his perfect face.

"You think what you did to me was funny?" I seethed.

"Not in the least. In fact, I think it hurt me more than it hurt you."

My jaw dropped. How could he say that?

"Asshole."

"Yes. But this asshole is attempting to keep you alive. Which he will. If you obey me. And since obedience appears to be a challenge for you, Miss Turner, I had to take measures. I hope the next time you have the sudden urge to defy my instructions, you'll think twice."

"Fuck you."

He laughed. "Perhaps next time. There's no better means to put a woman in her place."

My head whipped in his direction. "Not even you can believe that. Forcing yourself on a woman is barbaric."

"I never said I'd force you. However, I agree; rape is vile and savage, a coward's crime worthy of death."

He was implying that I might sleep with him willingly. Not a chance. That said, it was a strange relief to know that even King had his limits. And yet..."But apparently torture is okay, in your book?"

"Yes. A little pain is good for the soul. Reminds you you're alive and you should strive to remain that way. Fucking is also an effective reminder."

"Thanks," I said, "but I don't think I need to sleep with you to figure out that I don't want to die."

"I said fucking, not sleeping. However, given the men you've been with, I'm not surprised by your confusion. I doubt they had the courage to give you what you *really* wanted."

"Whoa. What's that supposed to mean? And how could you possibly know about the men I've slept with?" I seethed.

"I've been inside your head, Mia. I know everything. Even your darkest thoughts and desires." He scratched his chin as if contemplating. "I must admit, you surprised even me."

His words crashed right through me, igniting a painful tug-of-war inside my brain. It was like my mind insisted on pretending that none of these things were possible. People didn't get inside other people's heads. But it *was* possible. King had been there last night. I remember thinking how his being there hurt. I felt him scratching around, digging, like he'd been desperate to find something inside me. I remember silently screaming that what he wanted wasn't there, that it was tucked safely away inside my heart—a place he'd never enter.

I winced from the memory. "Don't, for one moment, mistake me for you, King. I have a soul."

"And I do not?" he asked, as if intrigued.

"Not a good one. I care what happens to people. You use them." I crossed my arms over my chest. "Must be a sad and lonely place inside that heart of yours."

He glanced at me from behind his mirrored lenses. "Perhaps you are right. But at the very least, I know who I am. You, on the other hand, are too frightened to face your true self." He looked at the road and grinned. "Such a shame because I find those dark bits very intriguing. I think I might like to ask them to come out and play." His grin grew even wider.

I hissed out a breath and shook my head. The man was egging me on. *Stay focused, Mia.* He'd said that he'd found Justin and the Artifact. If this was true, then all this could soon be over.

"What else did you say last night?" I asked.

King swerved through an intersection and ran the light.

I gripped the leather seat. "Shit. You're going to get us both killed."

"Not likely," he said coolly. "I told you that I learned the Artifact is here with your brother."

"How do you know that?" I asked.

"After we visited Vaughn in London, and I dropped you off at the hotel, I…" He hesitated. "I paid a visit to someone I've recently met. She has a particular tool for locating inanimate objects."

Did "tool" mean a gift? Damn. That sounded strange, but I didn't know what else to call it. "So they have a power or whatever?"

"Yes. The woman has a very special ability."

I quickly wondered if this woman could be a way out for me. Why would King need someone like me, who randomly saw crazy colors, when this woman could actually track objects?

"So you won't need me anymore," I said.

"I would not say that." Once again, he grinned. "Her abilities are hit and miss. Usually trackers, as we call them, lack any sort of precision. They can point you in a direction, like a compass, but that is all. Last night, she got lucky."

He made a turn down a long narrow street lined with warehouses, and I felt my temperature spike. My entire body tingled. "You're sure Justin is really here?"

I couldn't believe it.

King removed his glasses, and his eyes scanned the seemingly empty buildings with broken or boarded-up windows and covered in spray paint. "He was last night."

"Then why didn't you come last night?"

"I only knew he was in Edinburgh, so I had people scouring the city all night. I learned his exact location only twenty minutes ago."

People scouring the city. I gave that some thought. What sort of power and connections did a person have to have in order to mobilize a group of people large enough to cover an entire city? I guessed the answer was a lot. A lot of fucking power and connections.

He pulled up behind a broken-down-looking green sedan parked alongside a brick building. He exited the car, and I followed along. The nonstop drizzle immediately coated my hot face. We went down a narrow alley, toward the back of the building. A rusted metal door creaked as the wind nudged it open.

"Stay behind me, Mia."

What was King expecting to find? And why, for the love of God, was Justin hiding out in some abandoned warehouse in Edinburgh?

He pushed open the door and stepped inside. Dull light seeped inside the vacuous building from windows at the very tops of the high walls. The place looked like an abandoned factory stripped of all its machinery.

"I don't see anyone," I whispered.

King grabbed my hand, and I had to push myself to ignore how his powerful touch made me feel. He pulled me toward a small door in the far corner. It looked like it had been an office of some sort.

When we got to the door, he placed his ear against it, then turned and looked at me with those striking eyes. "Mia, this is one of those occasions where you must obey me." He placed his palm on my face, and his warmth overwhelmed my senses.

My body felt the urge to lean into him, to increase the contact. "Do you understand?"

I didn't. How could I be so absorbed in him? Now? With one simple touch?

I shook my head no.

He frowned. "Close your eyes. And do not open them again until I tell you to."

"What's wrong?" King was about to reach for my wrist, but I yanked my arm away. "Okay. I'm closing my eyes." I did as he asked, but only a moment passed, the space of three breaths.

"Fuck. You may open them now," King said.

"Why did you make me close them? What's wrong?" The last time King had me close my eyes, he killed two men.

King slipped his fingers inside the collar of his starched white shirt and pulled. "Dammit."

"What?" King didn't say anything, so I moved to open the door to the office.

He pulled me back. "Wait. You need to be prepared. It's not pleasant in there."

Oh no. No. "Please don't tell me he's dead."

"Your brother is not in there."

I didn't believe him. Why else would he be holding me back?

"Move, King." I pushed my way past him and shoved open the door. The muted light from the warehouse barely penetrated the dark, vacated room, but I saw a foot. A woman's bare foot sitting in a pool of blood.

Oh my God. "What happened to her?"

"Do I really need to explain?" King said all too casually.

I didn't respond to his snide comment because my thoughts instantly jumped to Justin.

I covered my mouth. "Is Justin okay? Where is he?"

"I do not know. But, Miss Turner, you must calm yourself and take a breath. I need you to look inside the room and tell me what you see." His gaze was intense and exacting.

"Some poor woman was murdered; we need to call the police."

King shook his head. "When are you going to learn, Miss Turner? The police cannot help her; she is dead. And if you'd like to help your brother, then you must step inside and tell me what you see."

I pushed out my palms. "Okay. Okay. Just let me catch my breath."

King closed his eyes, clearly holding back some sort of disapproval.

I sucked in a breath. "Okay. Ready."

I stepped inside the dark room, just a few inches from the woman's foot. At first, I could see only the blackness and that faint ray of light coming in through the door, but as I relaxed, the colors began to pop. I saw grays and greens, calm cool colors swirling about the walls.

"What do you see?" King asked impatiently.

"Nothing. Just…" My eyes wandered down to the woman. A thick ring of red encircled her body.

"Was the Artifact here?" he asked.

My eyes shifted away from the woman's torso. Across her palm was that distinct pattern I'd seen at the excavation site in Palenque. It was red and black, crisscrossing together.

"I think the woman had it," I said. "And…there are red blotches on the ground. They're shaped like footprints." I saw that they led out of the room. I followed them to where they faded into a giant red pool swirling on the ground just outside the door.

I gasped and held my hand over my face. "No. Please, no."

Before I could say another word, King had my hand and was pulling me out of there.

"Wait! Where are we going?" I pulled back. I wanted to keep looking for some sign of who it belonged to. "What does it mean—the red? Does it always mean somebody died in that spot? Is it Justin?"

King continued to yank me along, toward the exit.

"No! Goddammit!" I slipped from King's grip, and he looked about as surprised as I did. "Is that Justin's…" *Crap.* What should I call a pool of red light?

I wrapped my hands around my waist and took a deep breath. "Just tell me the truth, King. Did Justin die here? Is that what I just saw?" I didn't know if I could handle the truth or what it might do to me if Justin was dead, but I needed to know. "Please…tell me."

King looked down at me, and I think it was the first time I'd seen any sign of compassion touch those distant, cool gray eyes.

His mouth hardened into a straight line. "It could have been someone else. Justin could've run with the Artifact, which is why we must keep looking."

I tried to keep breathing, but wasn't sure I wanted to. "That's all you care about, isn't it?"

"Come. We need to leave before anyone shows up." King squeezed my shoulder.

"Why would they leave the woman but take the second body?"

"I don't know," he said quietly. "Whoever was here took the Artifact, and I need to track where it's going."

"The Artifact? The fucking Artifact, King? Are you kidding? My brother is probably dead. And they killed that poor woman in there! Yet, all you care about is some piece for your private collection?"

King was motionless, and I couldn't tell if he was about to walk away or do something to shut me up.

He stroked the short whiskers on the tip of his chin as if struggling with something. "You don't know that your brother is dead. And that 'poor woman' got what she deserved."

I blinked at him in shock.

"That was the woman who was tracking the Artifact for me," he explained.

"I don't understand," I said.

"She double-crossed me. I told her that if she located your brother, to stay out of sight. She obviously found your brother and the Artifact. And she obviously tried to make a deal of her own, probably to get the Artifact for herself. I won't waste my time feeling sorry for her."

"You won't feel sorry for her because she double-crossed you," I fumed. "You're serious? You think that's a reason someone should be murdered? You're a heartless, greedy son of a bitch."

His sublimely masculine face turned a deep shade of blistering red, and he closed the gap between us. "And you, Miss Turner, are a naïve, little girl. That woman is dead because of you. And if your brother was also killed, then his blood is also on your hands."

"How can you say that?"

"If you hadn't disobeyed me, I wouldn't have had to spend my time last night tracking you down and putting you somewhere safe instead of locating the Artifact. I would have gotten to your brother first."

His words stung. Was it because there was some truth to them?

"Make no mistake, Mia, if he's not dead already," King seethed, "your weakness *will* be the death of him."

I slapped his face, and his head whipped to the side.

King rubbed the spot on his cheek and smiled as if he'd almost enjoyed it. "You're lucky I still need you, Miss Turner."

"Do you, King? Do you really need me? Or is it want? I see the way you look at me. Is that what all this is about? Your little power trips and games to hurt me? Is it because I rejected you that first night?"

His nearly translucent eyes narrowed. "You would like to pretend that, now wouldn't you? But I believe it is the other way around. You're the one who regrets not getting fucked over that desk. You were too afraid to admit that those dark, uncivilized feelings exist inside you." His voice lowered to a menacing whisper. "But I know what's inside your head, Mia. I've seen everything."

"Then you know I hate you. That I'd rather be Vaughn's sex slave for the rest of my life than be your desktop fuckbuddy for one night."

His face turned into a cold, impenetrable fortress. He dipped his head. "I will try to remember that the next time the opportunity arises for a trade." He turned toward the door. "In the meantime, I have an artifact to hunt down, and if you want to find out what has happened to your pathetic, thieving brother, I suggest you keep your commitment to assist me."

He walked out of the building, and I stood there wanting to throw something at him. "Son of a bitch!" I marched after him, but he was gone. Poof. Not a sign of him in the street or anywhere.

I spun on my heel. *What the hell*? Where did he go?

Thank God his car was still there. I walked over, also grateful to see the keys in the ignition.

"Great." Well, he'd left me the car. And it did have GPS. But...I'd have to get back to the hotel on my own, driving on the left side of the road.

"Thanks, King. You are a real gentleman."

CHAPTER TWELVE

Accepting that Justin might be dead was my last and final mental straw. And perhaps King knew it. Because when I arrived back at the hotel, I had a message. King was sending me home until my services were again needed and to be at the airport in one hour. This time, Mack was waiting for me. Yes, he was alone, and he had a bruise on his cheek. When I asked what happened, he shook his head and simply said, "You. You happened."

I tried to ask if King had hit him because I'd gotten away in London, but Mack wouldn't talk to me. And when we stopped to refuel in New Jersey and present our passports, he barely breathed in my general direction.

"I'm sorry, Mack. I'm sorry for tricking you." I'd told him right before we were ready to take off for San Francisco.

"I'm not," he said. "King was right about you, and now I see it."

"What does that mean?" I asked.

Mack closed the cockpit door and kept to himself the entire flight.

Dammit. I felt bad. I really did. But what did Mack, or anyone for that matter, expect me to do? After everything that had happened in Mexico and London, the way I'd been treated, did Mack expect me to roll over and play nice? Seriously? Because clearly everyone was in it for themselves, and I was the only one actually concerned about helping Justin.

When we landed in San Francisco late Saturday night, I made one last attempt to apologize, but Mack was up and off as soon as the jet was in the hangar.

I sulked my way to the small private terminal, and then I realized I had no home to go to. I had no job. I had no hope. I had no...*brother.* I began to sob and dug my cell phone from my pocket. "Becca?"

"Shit, Mia. Where the hell have you been? Everyone's been going crazy looking for you."

I nodded and wiped the tears away. "I know. I know. I'm sorry. But...can you come and get me?"

"Where are you?" she asked.

"I'm at the airport."

"Don't move. I'll be there in twenty."

That night, I told Becca everything. She'd been my best friend since the second grade, and I thought that if anyone would believe me, Becca would. But when I saw the look in her eyes, I knew she not only questioned my sanity, she was heartbroken. I'd always told myself that Justin was the brother Becca never had, but her inconsolable tears told me he'd been much, much more than that. How had I not known? And it didn't matter if she believed the entire crazy story. Justin was still missing, and that was a fact not even she could argue with after I showed her the newspaper articles from Mexico.

I made her agree to wait to tell anyone until I dropped the bomb on my parents. Yes, I had to tell them. There was no more hiding. No more running from the horrible news of Justin being gone, perhaps forever.

Of course, they would get a version of the story that was limited to the tragedy surrounding Justin and his crew. I wouldn't mention King or the other crazy stuff. The less they knew about him, the better. He was dangerous, and God knew they wouldn't need any more pain in their lives.

After spilling my guts to Becca, she'd told me my parents had been calling everyone looking for me. When they learned I quit my job and moved out of my apartment without a word, it nearly sent my mother over the edge. What a shithead I was. How could I not have seen this coming?

I immediately called my mom, who proceeded to yell at me. I assured her I was fine and on my way back to San Francisco—a lie, to buy me some time—and that I would come to see them Monday night and explain everything. She was furious and relieved.

As for me, I needed to sleep. I was exhausted both mentally and physically.

I slept clear through Sunday, lost to the world until Becca woke me Monday morning at 5:30 a.m., making coffee.

She looked like she'd been hit by the same sad bus that had run me over.

"Are you sure you want to go to him?" she asked.

No. I didn't want to see King or go to his office. I wanted to mourn. I wanted to give in to my dark thoughts of Justin, but I couldn't allow that to happen. "What choice do I have?"

"You could call the police," she suggested.

"They can't help me, Becca. No one can. Trust me. I thought of every possible way to fix this, and there's only one thing I can do: move forward."

Becca nodded and sipped her coffee, leaning against the kitchen counter. "But this King guy sounds psycho, Mia. Who's to say he's not behind Justin's disappearance."

I'd thought about that, too. "No. He wants to find Justin as much as I do because he thinks he's got his Artifact."

She bobbed her head and looked at me with her wide, brown eyes. "This is crazy, Mia. Totally fucking crazy."

"Yeah. I know," I murmured. "But if I can find the Artifact, I can find Justin. Maybe get to him before anyone else does." And then what? Would I have to make another deal with King to buy Justin's protection?

"Please be careful, okay?"

"I will." I placed the half-empty cup in the sink.

"Good luck with your parents tonight. Call me as soon as you're done."

I flashed a pathetic little smile. "Thanks for everything."

"You're like a sister to me, Mia. I'm always here for you."

She left for work, and I dressed for a day in that cold, cold office: a warm blue sweater and jeans with black leather riding boots to keep out the rain. Another goddamned storm was hitting San Francisco. When I arrived at King's loft, it was still dark out, and I found the usual, unwelcoming chill of loneliness inside the empty space. No King. No customers. Only silence.

I took off my coat, turned on the lamp, and sat at the desk. I stared at my hands, wondering where all this would lead. How would it end?

Just as long as Justin is okay. That's all I ask. That would make this nightmare worth it.

The sound of a woman's giggle radiated from King's office.

I held my breath and listened. Another soft giggle and then the deep grumble of a male's voice.

Who was inside there? It couldn't be King because that man never showed up before 6:00 p.m. I got up and placed my ear to the door, trying to determine who it might be.

The door opened, and I stumbled forward, running right into King's large frame.

He caught me by the shoulders. "Miss Turner." His tone was as cold as his stunning eyes.

I straightened myself out and stepped back, catching a glimpse of the woman standing to my side. She looked...she looked...just like me.

Same height, same build, same wavy, blonde bob. Of course, her face was different, but she could have been my sister.

My jaw dropped.

"May I help you, Miss Turner?" King cocked his brow.

"Uh...no. Sorry. I just—just wasn't expecting you to be here."

King flashed that charming smile that worked on everyone except me. "It is my office. Who else would you expect?"

I ignored his question and walked back over to the desk, feeling like I'd been hit in the stomach. Why? I didn't know.

I watched King walk the woman to the door. And when she turned to say goodbye, he pulled her in close and kissed her hard. She melted into him and then sighed when he released her. It was exactly how he'd kissed me.

"Call me." She winked.

"As soon as I'm back in town," King replied and shut the door to the office.

"What the hell was that?" I asked.

King turned, and I finally noticed his appearance. His hair was completely mussed, his lips were red and puffy, his shirt was untucked from his pants, and his signature black tie hung around his neck.

"What was what?" he asked.

"You know *what*," I said.

He cocked his head to the side. "I think you know very well *what* that was."

I crossed my arms. "Actually, no. I don't."

"I fucked her. What's not to understand?" He headed for his office door, and I stood from the desk.

"Yeah. The sex part is pretty damned obvious. But you wanted me to see her. Why?"

He stopped in his doorway, with his back to me. "After Edinburgh, I did not think you would be here. And who I fuck is my own damned business."

Why was I so angry? I didn't know. I just—I just was. "That's bullshit. She looked like me. You were trying to make a point. What was it? That I'm replaceable. That you can find a new Mia anytime you like? One that won't break or disobey you? Are you hoping I'd get jealous?"

King turned and leaned casually against his office doorway. "Those are all fascinating hypotheses. But I'm sorry to tell you that none are correct."

More of his head games. I picked up a pen from the desk and threw it at him. Of course, the bastard had animal-like reflexes and caught it in midair.

I growled. "Call me when you're ready to stop playing head games and help me find out what happened to my brother."

I grabbed my stuff and headed for the door, berating myself every step of the way for allowing him to get under my skin.

"He's not dead," King blurted.

I stopped and looked back at him. "How do you know?"

King lifted his dark brows.

"You're not going to tell me, are you?" I fumed. "Will you at least tell me where he is?"

King crossed his arms. "I don't know. I've got people searching for him, but it would go a lot faster if I had another tracker."

"Is there anything I can do?" I asked.

"Just go home. I'll call if I have need of you."

I was being dismissed like his servant. "Thanks to you, I no longer have a home." I left, but I could swear King's eyes were on me every step of the way to Becca's. I even smelled him in the air and felt his breath on my face. But there was no one there. I saw only the early morning city traffic and people walking to work. No King.

I'm losing my mind. Or perhaps I wasn't.

I spent the rest of the day alone at Becca's apartment, doing what I could to pick through all of the newspaper articles related to Justin and his team. Everything was written in Spanish, making the task long and arduous.

Still, I had to believe there would be something there to tell me more, some sort of indication of what that Artifact was or why Justin would get mixed up with these people for it. Perhaps there'd be some clue as to where he'd gone or other parties involved. Sadly, I found nothing apart from two articles which said the exact same thing about the team being kidnapped. No follow-up. No leads.

Those poor, poor families. I needed to talk to King about tipping off the local authorities. Those men's families needed to know the truth. Or maybe I could contact the families directly, I thought. Perhaps send an anonymous tip.

I tried to look up more information about the team: names, where they were from, etc., but again, didn't find much. That is, until I found an article regarding the site's discovery and that an American team would be leading the excavation. It said the work was being funded by a private company based out of the U.K.

Could Vaughn have been the backer? It might explain why my brother had gone to London and why Guzman had told me that Vaughn wanted his things returned.

I was just about to give up for the day and head over to my parents' house, but decided to look up one more thing: Seer of Light.

I entered the term into the search window, but only came up with a bunch of hits for a character from some fantasy role-playing game. The woman held a cocked bow and arrow and wore a sort of Viking-looking outfit.

I hissed. *Silly.* Why did I think I'd learn anything on Google? Whatever this "gift" was, I somehow knew that King would be the only one to have answers. For a price, of course.

I looked up at the clock, and it was almost six. "Crap." I closed Becca's laptop and grabbed my purse. I made a quick check in the mirror and confirmed that I did, in fact, look like shit. I quickly smoothed on some powder and lipstick and finger-combed my messy blonde mop. My mother was never the superficial type, but looking like I was about to die of some horrible illness wouldn't ease her worrying.

As soon as I got outside, the rain began to pick up again, making it once more difficult to hail a cab. I seriously missed my centrally located apartment. Becca lived all the way over in the Marina District.

Thirty minutes later, I was finally at my parents' door. I rang, and they buzzed me in.

"Here goes," I mumbled to myself as I made my way upstairs to their living room, but no one was there.

"Mom?" I called out.

"We're in the kitchen, honey."

I noticed the sound of laughter almost immediately, and when I entered, I couldn't believe who I saw.

What the hell is he doing here? My jaw dropped.

My mother's blue eyes lit up. "Oh, Mia! Honey." She popped up from the kitchen table and gave me a hug, but my eyes didn't move from the exquisite man in the expensive black suit with the hypnotic light-gray eyes sitting at her table, enjoying a cup of tea. "It's so nice to see you, baby."

"Uhhh. Nice to see you, too," I said.

"Mia," she turned toward the intruder, "this is Mr. King. He works with your brother's organization."

What the *hell* was going on? I almost lost the strength in my legs. Was this yet another dream?

"I go by King. Just—King," he corrected her.

"Oh. Kind of like Madonna or Cher?" I said, fuming. *How dare he be here!*

King shot me a look.

Just then, my father entered the kitchen, wearing a blue golf shirt, holding a bottle of scotch. "Ah. Here's the good stuff." He looked up and saw me. "Mia, good, you're here."

"What's going on?" I asked.

My father was the first to chime in. "I think you should sit, Mia." He hitched up his navy blue slacks and cleared his throat.

I looked at him, then my mother, and finally King, who had a smirk in his eyes. Yes. In his goddamned eyes, of all things.

I sat, trembling every inch of the way.

"Mia," my father placed the bottle at the center of the kitchen table, "I know this will be a shock, but your brother has been lying to us."

King had told them? "Yeah, I know," I replied.

My mother smiled. "You do? Oh, honey. I think it's great. What your brother is doing for his country is…well, we couldn't be prouder."

I blinked. "I think I've missed something."

King cleared his throat. "Mia, my name is King. I came here tonight to tell your parents about your brother's work with us."

"You did?" I asked.

"Obviously, the fact that he's been working with the government is not to be shared, but we thought you and your family needed to know why he's been out of touch for so long."

I swallowed down a glob of rage in my throat. "Wow. That is a shock." *What the ever-loving hell is going on?*

King flashed a glance at his watch—or had he just looked at the tattoo on his wrist?—and quickly rose from the table. His imposing stature and authoritative presence filled my mother's kitchen. "Well, it was a pleasure meeting Justin's family." He threw a business card on the table. "If you have any questions, don't hesitate to call. However, Justin should be in touch in a few weeks."

I scooped up the card immediately and shoved it in my jeans pocket. I had questions. Lots of questions. Such as, what the hell was he doing at my parents' house, serving up a giant, heaping pile of bullcrap?

"Oh, but I thought you were going to stay," said my father. "I really wanted to hear more about these drug cartels."

King flashed one of his signature charming smiles, and I could swear I saw my mother catch her breath as if entranced by the beautiful man.

Oh my God. King was using one of his little mind tricks on them. That's why they were so happy to swallow his story.

"Perhaps next time. But I have an important meeting to attend." King dipped his head. "Pleased to meet you, Mia."

I rose from the chair and was about to follow him out, but my mother wasn't having it. "Just where do you think you're going, Mia? You have a lot of explaining to do."

"I, uhhh, was going to show King to the door. Be right back."

I followed King down the stairs, ready to unleash a fury, but as soon as we stepped onto the front porch, he swung around and grabbed my wrist. He firmly held his palm over my tattoo. "Before you commence, Miss Turner, what I anticipate will be a colorful display of unhappy words, I want you to listen."

Son of a bitch wants me to listen? I'll kill him!

"Mia." His voice was low as he stared deeply into my eyes. "Just listen." He released my wrist, and I instantly felt my control return.

"What are you doing here?" I asked.

"Stopping you from making a big mistake."

"*What?*" I barked.

He held out his hand. "I know what you were going to tell your parents tonight."

"How did you know?"

He narrowed his eyes. "I think you are aware, Miss Turner, that some of the abilities I've acquired do not come with a 'how,' they simply are what they are."

More of his creepy bullshit. I wondered if his ability to listen to my conversations was linked to my tattoo. Why the hell not? He was able to track me with it and evoke a hypnotic-like suggestive state in me just by touching it.

"Mia!" I heard my mother call.

I sighed. "Why are you here, King?" I whispered.

"Because telling your parents the truth, when you do not know the truth, would only cause them suffering. And I cannot afford to have you distracted, thinking about their well-being, wanting to be by their sides to console them when we have work to finish."

"You mean finding your stupid Artifact."

"Mia!" my mother called out again.

I sighed. "I need to go."

King's lips twitched into that little half-grin he made sometimes, and his eyes flashed to my lips.

"What?" I asked.

"I find it fascinating that you're afraid of your parents, but not me."

I rolled my eyes. "Why's that fascinating?"

"Because I terrify the hell out of everyone else. And they are right to be afraid." He turned and made his way down the short flight of steps leading off the porch onto the sidewalk. "I will send Arno to your friend Becca's home in two hours. Pack light."

No. Not again. "I think we're pretty much done."

"We are not done until I say we're done."

I glared. "Is that all you got?"

His eyes narrowed for a moment, and then he scratched his chin. I think he was debating his next move. "Did you not just come to my office and ask how you could help?"

"Yes, but—"

"There is new information."

"Are you going to share it?"

"No."

Of course not. Because it would totally ruin his whole mysterious vibe. Can't have that.

"Then you're on your own. And, by the way, we need to talk." I wanted to ask him what he knew about Justin's financial backers and also convince him to tip off the authorities regarding the horrible fate of Justin's team. The families needed to know because the pain of not knowing had to be tearing them to pieces.

"We can talk on the plane," he said, not bothering to turn around or stop walking.

"I'm not going!" I protested as he walked away. "And you can't force me forever."

King waved into the air. "You'll enjoy the trip. I promise."

"Not going!"

My mother called for me again, and I gritted my teeth as King disappeared down the dark wet sidewalk.

I took a calming breath and made my way back up to the kitchen. Now I had no idea what I was going to tell them about why I'd vacated my apartment, quit my job, and left town without a word.

I guess it's your turn to make up a big fat juicy lie.

⊱⚬⚬⚭⚬⊰

Having received the biggest chewing out of my life for hiding "the truth," not asking for their help, and losing my dream job because of my "irresponsible and stubborn ways," I called Becca the moment I left my parents' house.

Not only did I need to update her on the turn of events, regarding what they'd been told about Justin and my situation, but I needed to warn her that a rather large, unfriendly foreign gentleman would be showing up at any moment at her house to collect me.

"Mia?" Becca answered on the first ring. "How'd it go?"

"Like shit. You're not going to believe it, but—"

"King showed up, lied to them, and told you to be ready by eight thirty?"

"How did you know?" I asked, terrified by how she might answer.

"Because…it's 8:45, and he's here right now, waiting for you."

Huh? Dammit. I had the urge to throw my cellphone on the cement. "And he told you all that?"

"Yeah. He said that I needed to know how important keeping your parents in the dark was. That if I wanted to save Justin, I had to lie, too."

He'd manipulated Becca. I just couldn't believe it. I wanted to scream at the top of my goddamned lungs.

"You're going tonight, right, Mia?" she asked.

Oh my frigging God. "Can you put him on, please?"

I heard the muffled voice of Becca say, "She wants to talk to you. Can I get you a refill on that coffee?"

I heard King's deep voice reply, "You are too kind, Becca. But I'm fine." There was a quick pause. "Hello, Mia."

"Son of a bitch. What did you do to Becca? Did you brainwash her? Use your weird sadistic powers on her? Because so help me—"

"I did no such thing."

"What in God's name are you doing there, King?"

"I thought I'd try a more subtle approach with you."

"Subtle? You show up at my parents' house, lie to them, and now you're manipulating Becca. Leave her out of this."

"You are the one who pulled her in by sharing facts that were not yours to share."

How did he know that I'd told Becca everything? *Shit.* Probably the same way he knew I was going to my parents' house that evening to tell them about Justin. Had the man bugged her apartment? Or, an even more horrifying thought, maybe he really was inside my head. All. The. Time.

"What do you want from me?" I asked.

"For you to get on a plane and attend a party in Los Angeles tonight."

"You want me to go with you to a party tonight?" Was he out of his mind?

"No," he replied, "not with me. I cannot attend. In fact, that is why I'm here now, to explain there is a change of plans. But as usual, you're late, and had you arrived on time, you would see the look on my face is one of respectful insistence."

Respectful insistence. "You mean, you're asking me?" I continued walking down the steep hill toward one of the main avenues to catch a cab back to Becca's.

"Yes, I'm asking. In an assertive manner, but I'm asking."

King was asking. How odd. It definitely piqued my curiosity. "Who's throwing the party?"

"10 Club."

"You're joking. Why the hell would I want to go to a party with your billionaire yachting buddies?"

"I do not own a yacht," he said blandly. "I own an ocean freighter line."

Sure. Of course. "Why do you want me to go?"

"I need your help, and helping me is always in your best interest."

I wanted to tell him to take a long hike down a deep, dark hole, but the fact that he was asking— not forcing—made me wonder. King never asked. He demanded.

"Will going help find Justin?"

"Yes or no, Miss Turner?" he replied impatiently.

Again, I wondered why King was asking when we both knew he could force me. Was this some sort of olive branch? "Fine. I'll go."

"Very good, Miss Turner. I will leave instructions on the plane. I will see you as soon as I'm able. And, Miss Turner?"

"Yes?"

"Do not deviate in any way from my instructions, and do not leave Mack's sight tonight. Not for a second."

Oh, goody. That sounded promising.

CHAPTER THIRTEEN

When I finally returned to Becca's apartment, Arno
was indeed waiting to take me straight to the
airport, and Becca already had several of her
dresses laid out for me on the bed. Most of my
clothes were in storage.

"I can't believe you fell for King's bullcrap,
Becca," I said, shoving my makeup and hair
products into a small overnight bag.

She shrugged. "I didn't 'fall' for anything, Mia.
His argument made sense; that's all." She held up a
blue dress. "How's this one?"

I pointed to a sleeveless, black dress. I hoped it
would be nice enough. "He's dangerous. Didn't you
hear a word I said about him? He killed people right
in front of me."

"Okay. But didn't you say those men were about
to attack you?"

I slipped on the dress, and she zipped up the
back. "Yeah, but—"

"Sounds to me," she said, "like King is just the sort of man who can save Justin from whatever shit he's mixed up in."

Dammit. I didn't have time to debate Becca on the merits of King. The man was bad news.

She reached down in her closet and handed me a pair of black strappy heels. "Take these." My foot was about a half size smaller than hers, but they fit.

"How do I look?" I couldn't believe I had agreed to go to this crazy party.

Becca looked me over. "Lose the bra and underwear. I can see everything."

I slipped them off and then held out my arms. "Now?"

"You look nervous."

"That's because I am."

And, call me even crazier, but I was just as nervous about seeing Mack again as I was going to this mysterious event. He hadn't been very happy with me the last time we'd seen each other only two days ago—not nearly enough time for his anger to dissipate. Now, the angry man would be my date. And my bodyguard.

"Use the clear deodorant and lots of it," she suggested.

"Thanks." I grabbed my bag; I'd do my hair and makeup on the plane. "Wish me luck."

"You don't need luck. You just need King." I wanted to throttle her. Literally throttle her. What the hell did she know about King? For the love of God, she'd seen the tattoo and had heard every gory detail of my month. Didn't she get that the man was the devil or, at the very least, some evil sorcerer from the dark ages, sent forward in time to destroy me?

Really, Mia. Really? Why don't you call Gandalf and ask him to loan you his staff to fight King off?

"King is dangerous, Becca. Stay the hell away from him."

"Mia Turner, I think you're actually jealous."

What the...ugh! I shook my head, bit my tongue, and headed out the door.

When I arrived at the jet, I spotted Mack in his pilot's uniform outside, checking the gear. I don't know what caught my attention, exactly, but maybe it was the intense look on his face as he surveyed the plane, clipboard in hand, that boyish expression nowhere to be found. In that moment, I could easily visualize him in some sort of military garb, camouflaged face to match his clothes, black boots, night vision goggles, jumping out of a plane over enemy territory. He seemed fearless, competent, and loyal. I still couldn't understand why a man like that would work for King. Who had King found for him?

Mack caught me staring. I waved to him, and he jerked his head in my direction. I took that as a sign his anger towards me had improved.

I trudged my way up the Jetway steps, and it dawned on me how, under alternative circumstances, flying around on a private plane with a hot pilot would be cool. As would seeing a giant rectangular box with my name on it sitting on the front row of seats. In said box was a horribly expensive, satin red gown with intricate red crystal beading. It was a red-carpet-worthy Valentino.

"Uh. Wow?" was about all I could say when I held it up. The strapless, tapered bodice started with a push-up bustline and hugged its way down to the hips, where it flared out, giving it an upside-down trumpet shape. A deep slit up the middle would certainly show off my legs. It was elegant and sexy and—

"Like the dress?" Mack stood just inside the jet's doorway.

"Yeah. Sure. I just wish I knew why we're going to this party." And how it would help me find out what happened to Justin.

He slipped an envelope from his pocket. "Here are your instructions."

"I feel like *La Femme Nikita.* Do I get a gun to strap to my thigh?"

Mack shrugged his brows. "Just what we need: Mia with a gun."

"What? I'm sure I could handle one. I went to the arcade when I was younger. Point and shoot."

Mack smirked and flashed a little bit of that soft underbelly I found so appealing. "Uh, yeah. That's what I'm afraid of. You, your temper, and the pointing and shooting."

I laughed.

He removed his pilot's hat and finger-combed his blonde hair. His fierceness moved down another notch. "Besides, you won't need a gun. You'll have me."

"And…you're carrying a gun?"

"I don't need one."

Why the hell not? I wondered. Before I could ask my question, he shoved the envelope at me.

"Stop asking so many questions and read the letter, Nikita."

As soon as I was strapped into my seat, Mack had us cleared for takeoff, down the runway, and into the air. I held the letter in my hand the entire time, almost too afraid to read it. That's when my arm started to tingle. I looked at the intricate "K" design and stroked the skin, wondering how King could use it to track and control me.

I didn't know, but the thing had power, and it was not my imagination. Even then, as I touched the mark with my palm, weird prickles blossomed over my body as if King were right there, standing over me with his menacing frame and strikingly handsome face.

I closed my eyes and again felt his breath tickle my cheek, as if he were leaning down to whisper in my ear. "Read the fucking letter, Miss Turner."

I gasped and looked around. The cabin was completely empty.

You're obsessed with him, Mia. Don't let him get inside your head.

Right. A little too late for that.

I begrudgingly tore open the envelope and read:

Miss Turner,

Once again, my apologies for being unable to attend the event in person. I will, however, be there in spirit, and Mack will ensure your safety. You are to stay by his side throughout the evening, and under no circumstances are you to speak to anyone unless Mack requests it of you.

However, should anyone insist you engage with them, you are to simply tell them you are mine. I understand that this may sound repugnant to a woman such as yourself, but I am confident your ego will survive the tarnish.

I lifted my eyes from the letter to digest the words. What sort of frigging party would this be? I couldn't speak to anyone, and if they spoke to me, I was only allowed to say that I belonged to King?

I steadied my hand and returned to reading.

Do not let the civilized appearance of the attendees deceive you, Miss Turner. They are anything but. They are savages, above any law, and they live only by the code of "might makes right."

While you are there, Mack will be acquiring new resources on my behalf. You are to use your abilities to sweep the room.

You know what to look for.

Stay out of trouble.

— K

I blew out a breath and mentally chewed. Basically, it sounded like I'd be going to a party of Kings. Lots and lots of mean, dangerous, civilized-only-on-the-outside Kings.

"This ought to be fun," I mumbled to myself. I grabbed the dress and headed to the bathroom. The dress fit my frame like a glove, as if it had been hand-sewn for my curvy body, right down to the way it pushed up my breasts. King had even managed to procure a pair of slinky red Valentino heels to go with it. Yeah, they fit perfectly, too. Yeah, it creeped me out.

My hair was its usual challenge, so instead of trying to tame the blonde beast, I teased it out a little to give it that wild bohemian look. After throwing on some red lipstick and covering up the circles under my eyes, I had to admit, I didn't look half bad for someone that had been through what I had in only seven days.

I shook my head in the mirror and braced myself on the sink. Seven days. Had it really only been seven days? I'd been detained and threatened in Mexico, tattooed by some eccentric, medieval billionaire—King—discovered I had a sixth sense, seen a ghost and a dead body, been taken to London, almost stolen by a serial killer who trafficked humans, saw King kill two guys, ran off to Edinburgh, saw another dead body, and had basically lost all hope I'd ever find my brother. "You're still standing, girl. Don't you forget it." And when this was all over, because there was no way in hell I would stay with King forever, I'd write a damned book about this nightmare. Fiction, of course.

I stepped out of the bathroom and ran right into Mack. His normally disheveled hair was combed back, and he wore a very expensive-looking tuxedo. The man looked frigging gorgeous.

He stilled, and his eyes swept over my body—head to toe and back again. He swallowed. "You look, uhhh—nice."

I swallowed, too. "You clean up pretty well, yourself."

A bit of playfulness flickered in his blue eyes. "If you like this, just wait until you see me tune up the jet's engine. Grease monkey is my best look."

I smiled. I liked this version of Mack.

"I'm glad you're not mad at me anymore, Mack."

"No worries. I have a temper, but I get over things quickly. I'm not big on grudges."

"Is that what happened to your face? Your temper?" Mack still had that bruise on his cheek, obviously.

"King and I had a little disagreement over who should retrieve you after you took off in London. He won."

That made me feel like complete crap. "I'm really sorry, Mack. I didn't mean to cause you problems. I was afraid. I still am."

He stared at me for a quiet moment and then shook his head. "I, uh," he forced himself back to Serious Mack, "just wanted to tell you we'll be landing soon. Time to strap in."

"Thanks. I'm all ready to go."

"Read the letter?" he asked.

"Yep. I am to be seen and not heard."

His eyes swept over my body once again. Then he shook his head.

"What?" I asked.

Mack's eyes flashed to my cleavage. "I don't know what the hell King was thinking putting you in that dress. That's like marinating you in blood, then dropping you in a shark tank."

Dammit. I knew going to this party was a mistake. "I thought I'd be safe with you."

"You'll be safe, but it's just going to take me a hell of a lot more effort."

"But you were some sort of assassin type, special-forces-whatever, right?" Honestly, I knew nothing about the military other than the basics: army, navy, air force, and marines.

"I was a navy fighter pilot for a few years. Then I moved to a special assignment. I don't like to talk about it."

That last part of his comment made me wonder why. Maybe something bad happened to him.

Mack looked me over again. "Sometimes I think King does this sort of shit just because he likes to keep me on my toes."

"Ya think?" I smiled. It was funny to hear Mack call King on his BS antics. And it was good to know I wasn't the only one who objected.

"Yeah. I think." He glanced over his shoulder. "I gotta land the plane. Just try to relax tonight and…"

He scratched his unshaved chin with a day's worth of golden-brown growth.

"What?"

"And don't fuck it up."

I watched his elegantly dressed, broad back disappear into the cockpit. "Thanks."

Within the hour, Mack and I were down on the ground and into a black stretch limo. I felt like we were living on some twisted reality show where everything looked like a spectacular Cinderella-like dream on the outside, when really, it was the story of *Dante's Inferno*.

"So, where are we going?" I asked.

"Bel Air."

I hadn't been to Bel Air, but I knew it had the most expensive homes in L.A. Who hadn't watched *The Fresh Prince*? "And who's throwing the party?"

"The host is more or less the president of 10 Club."

They had a president?

"Only," Mack added, "no one holds any allegiance to him. This is pretty much his only function."

"Having a party?" I asked.

"Consider this like a swap meet."

Now I was lost.

"I thought this was a party," I said.

"It looks like a party, but really, it's an annual event where people of like interests barter for things they need. It's also an excuse to get together, check out any new members."

My mind started to add up all of those tiny crumbs that had been left in my bed, digging under my skin. Vaughn and King trying to barter for me and the Artifact. King mentioning he collected "things" and acquired certain "abilities." The strange secretiveness. And the bizarre code of ethics King seemed to live by—thou shall obey me, I am your master, etc. It was like he didn't live in this world, but in some uber-wealthy alternate reality.

"10 Club isn't just a club for billionaires," I realized aloud.

Mack nodded. "So King told you?"

"No, not exactly. I'm just figuring it out."

"I heard you're good at that," Mack said.

"That and running away, getting myself knee-deep in shit I don't understand, and occasionally hanging with people I shouldn't."

He chuckled. "How about following people you shouldn't? Is it true? Did you really follow King the first day you two met?" he asked.

I nodded.

"Your balls are bigger than I thought," he said. "I've seen King kill for less."

"Doesn't it bother you to work for someone like that?"

Mack looked at me and tilted his head, grinning. "Who's to say I haven't done the same?"

"Have you?"

He looked away. "I've done many things that would shock you, Mia."

"You didn't answer my question."

He looked at me, and I caught a glimpse of his pensive face as a car passed by. "I'd kill for him, and he'd do the same for me."

I had the feeling that what Mack really meant was they already had. "What exactly did King do for you?" I just couldn't figure out how someone like Mack could be so happy working for a sadistic bastard like King.

"He…" Mack took a shallow breath, "acquired me. At a party like this one, actually."

"What the hell?"

"It's a long story. All I can say is that after I served in Iraq, I wasn't the same person. I did things I'm not proud of and got mixed up with someone who took advantage of me."

How anyone could take advantage of a man like Mack boggled my mind.

"Who?" I asked.

"Doesn't matter. But they weren't kind to me. Once the fog began to clear, I knew I needed to get away. King helped me."

So Mack had been looking for his freedom from someone. That was the deal he made with King.

I sighed to myself. "How does someone 'acquire' another person?" It was morally repugnant.

"The world is full of some sick people. As for 10 Club, once you make a deal with any of them, you're in for life. They own you, just like King owns you."

"He doesn't own me," I protested.

"You really believe that?"

Yes, I did.

"So," I said, "you're trying to tell me this 10 Club is really some secret society of demented, wealthy people who go around making deals, 'acquiring' people, and then trading them like baseball cards?"

"No. They are a group of very rich, very powerful people who *collect* things, all kinds of things. To some it's a game—entertainment. To others, it's about power—the more, the better. And some play because they genuinely need something."

"*Need.* Like what?"

He shrugged. "Couldn't tell you. No one wears their true intentions on their sleeves. Anything you care about is a weakness, and the members will exploit it if they figure out what it is."

Frigging insanity! Was he serious?

"But we're going there tonight looking for something; won't they know what we want?" I asked.

"Not really. You could be trading for something that someone else wants. Most of the time, you could care less about the things you're negotiating for. It's a means to an end."

This was some crazy, messed-up stuff. And in some ways, it explained why King was such a cold, calculating, heartless person. Or had he always been that way and then found his flock? I didn't know, but now I knew why he had no qualms about using my weakness—Justin—to barter for something he wanted: me. Or my services, anyway.

"I can't believe this," I whispered.

"Believe it."

"Who would be insane enough to dream this up? To start an entire society like this?" I asked.

Mack shrugged. "It's been around for a very, very long time. Some say it dates back six hundred years."

"So King, he wants the Artifact. Is it because he really wants it, or is he trying to trade for something else?"

"What the hell do I care?" Mack asked. "I show up when I'm needed. I don't get involved in the why."

Funny. Mack didn't care about the why, and King didn't care about the how. They were perfect for each other. Like peanut butter and jelly.

"What about this?" I pointed to my wrist. "And what about all of the other crazy crap I've seen?"

It went way beyond a psycho group of rich people bartering for whatever-the-hell.

Mack looked uneasy, almost...well, pissed off. "It means you're off the table. Permanently."

"Sorry?"

"King has branded you. No one can make a play for you. It's against the rules."

There are rules?

"Mack? Why are you telling me all this?"

"King asked me to."

More conflict. King wanted me to know what lie hidden behind the curtain, which meant he was showing me trust. But knowing that you're only a foot away from the deadly grip of a monster's sharp teeth wouldn't bring you a good night's sleep.

"Why didn't he tell me himself?" I asked.

"He felt the truth might be better received if it came from me."

"Oh." I seemed to be saying that a lot lately. But what else could I say? "Yippee" and "super-duper" weren't really options.

"I'm sure I don't need to point out that sharing this information with anyone on the outside would require your immediate execution," Mack said remorsefully. "There are only a handful of rules. That's one of them, too."

For some strange reason, I wasn't surprised. "And the other rules?"

"King didn't approve my sharing those. You'll have to ask him yourself. Ah. We're here." Mack straightened his bow tie and then looked at me. The limo pulled up behind a long line of flashy cars.

Oh no. This was it. I must've looked like I'd been hit by a very large, heavy vehicle, perhaps carrying a load of bricks.

Mack reached out and squeezed my hand. "You'll be okay, Mia. You can handle this."

"Sure." I just needed to…needed to…

I bolted from the limo to throw up in a hedgerow. Nothing came out. A few people passed by and stared, but I was mostly hidden in the bushes.

"Mia?" Mack gripped my shoulders from behind. "Are you all right?"

I straightened myself up, and he handed me a handkerchief. Lucky me, it was tux night, so he'd had one handy.

"Thanks." I blotted underneath my eyes and wiped my mouth. "Just nerves, I think."

Mack looked down at me with his wide blue eyes. "Just focus on breathing, smiling, and doing whatever you Seers do."

It was the first time someone besides King had mentioned my "ability." In all honesty, I had been doing everything in my power to ignore the whole thing. It made me uneasy to have a skill I didn't understand, but as King rightly pointed out, there'd be time for figuring out the "how" later.

"Okay." I focused on the sensation of my lungs expanding, and we proceeded down the long walkway toward the ostentatious, English Tudor-style mansion.

When we got to the entrance, there was a line of ten or so couples, each greeting a man at the door.

"No," I gasped. It was Vaughn. "This is *his* party?" I stopped in my tracks.

Mack gently pushed the small of my back. "Don't worry. It will be fine."

"But King killed his men. They were going to take me."

Mack whispered in my ear and nudged me closer to the door. "Vaughn won't touch you. Just stay with me."

Vaughn shook hands with the couple in front of us, an older bald gentleman with a plump redhead who appeared to be his wife. Vaughn didn't look at all like the uncivilized, greasy sleazeball I'd seen back in London. He wore a traditional tuxedo and had actually brushed his thinning silver hair.

Regardless of his civilized exterior, however, I knew a monster lived inside, and I began to wonder if everyone at the party was just as bad as him. And to think, these were people with money and influence. No wonder the world was so messed up.

Vaughn ushered the older couple inside and wished them success in finding whatever they were looking for. When his eyes settled on Mack and me, his slithery smile melted away.

"Ah, Mr. Taylor. Nice of you to join us. Welcome." But his beady brown, cataract-filled eyes said the opposite.

Mr. Taylor. That was Mack's last name? I supposed it fit, but I felt irritated learning it from Vaughn. I should have asked him myself. What was it with me and names?

Mack shook his hand. "King sends his regards. He's tied up on some important business, but asked me to tell you that he looks forward to seeing you soon." Mack leaned in and spoke quietly. "He says to wish you luck; you'll need it." Mack smiled combatively and shrugged his brows.

So cocky.

Vaughn dipped his head. "And tell King that I look forward to seeing him, too. He'll be the biggest find for my collection yet."

Okay. So apparently this entire conversation was code for "Come and get me, muthafucka" and "Oh. I'm comin', all right. Your ass is mine."

What I didn't understand was why Vaughn would see King as a prize of some sort or how he possibly believed he could "acquire" such a determined, ruthless SOB.

Good luck with that one, Vaughn.

Vaughn turned toward me and took my right hand. "Miss Veronica, so we meet again."

His touch sent icy shivers shooting through my arm, but I willed myself not to react. When his lips touched the top of my hand, however, my vision became tinted with blood red. I pulled my hand away. I had to.

Vaughn didn't react, but I could see the displeasure flickering in his soulless eyes.

"Vaughn, may I introduce *Mia Turner*," Mack said. "She belongs to King."

Vaughn didn't flinch but his reaction, a glance at my left wrist, tipped off his surprise. Fearful that Vaughn might lash out at me, I was about to step back when he laughed. "Tell King that we'll settle up later." He gestured toward the inside of the house. "Have a pleasant evening, Mr. Taylor and Miss Turner. I hope you find what you're looking for."

I was only too happy to escape the presence of Vaughn, but entering his home created another sort of angst. I felt like I was entering a party for Hannibal Lectors searching for their next depraved prize to mutilate and devour.

Mack escorted me inside, where we were immediately greeted by a waiter serving champagne in the foyer. Mack began scanning the elegantly dressed crowd milling about in the enormous white living room.

"This is really Vaughn's house?" I whispered to Mack while my eyes took in the brightly colored Warhols and Lichtensteins on the walls.

He nodded. "He's got nice taste for a psychopath, doesn't he?" I tried not to think about that man's "hobby" or what he did to people once he added them to his collection.

We made our way through the living room, and I happily played the part of quiet arm candy. I wanted zero interaction with these people. And every time someone shook my hand, I tried to get a look at their palms. I didn't see what I was looking for— any sign of the Artifact—and apparently, neither did Mack.

Mack said, "Let's go outside."

We walked out the patio doors into the brick-paved garden. Paper lamps strung on long white runners gave the garden a peaceful wedding reception-like appearance. People stood gathered around small, circular tables, smoking cigars, drinking, and enjoying themselves.

One man with thick glasses and perfectly combed blond hair had a huge crowd congregated around him.

"That guy looks familiar," I said. "Do I know him from somewhere?"

"He's a congressman."

What? I polished off my champagne and grabbed another from a waiter passing by. "What does he collect?"

"He's a powerbroker. See all of those people with him?"

I nodded and sipped my champagne.

"Most of them are either politicians or owners of big companies."

Mack nodded to another group, mostly men, mostly older, all smoking cigars and standing in a circle. "Those guys are into women. Pretty women."

"Hookers?" I asked. Maybe that was King's clique.

"No. Movie stars, aristocrats, only A-listers. Vaughn does a lot of transactions within that group."

Holy crap. Just then, Ashlee Randall and Mai Ling Choo, two extremely famous actresses, strolled by sipping martinis.

Mack reached out and gave his head a little shake, cautioning me not to stare. But how could I not? They'd both received Oscars this year. They were beautiful and glamorous. Why would they be part of this depravity?

"Mia." He cautioned me again.

I sighed quietly and nodded, trying to recall what I'd been saying.

Oh yes. "Why did Vaughn want me?"

"King told him you were the illegitimate daughter of some Russian prince."

Okay. So Vaughn liked high-end trophy women. "I thought no one was supposed to know what everyone else collected," I asked.

"Most of these things are for fun, for socializing, like belonging to a golf or tennis club. The real cutthroat deals, what people are really after, are kept close to the vest, but everyone has suspicions."

"What about King?" I asked. "What's his hobby? Power, women?"

"King doesn't need more power, and I've never seen him want to be with a woman longer than one night."

"If that's the case, what's he in this for?" I couldn't help but sweep the crowd again with my eyes. There were so many familiar-looking people.

No! Ten feet away, two very well-known tech CEOs conversed with an Arab man. Was that one of the Sauds, I wondered?

That's when I began to realize that 10 Club wasn't just some underground social club for billionaires with illicit and depraved fetishes.

"You'll have to ask him," Mack replied. "I don't know. And I don't care. But he seems to deal more with the less traditional types of commodities."

"Such as?" I asked.

"The occult, as you've seen firsthand."

Two slender brunettes in their forties walked out to the patio and caught several looks from the crowd. Mack immediately noticed them, too. "There they are."

Mack and I approached the women. They both wore long black dresses and were about as thin as sipping straws. Their faces had that overdone, addicted-to-plastic surgery look.

"Good evening, ladies."

Both women ogled Mack like that delicious candy bar they'd obviously been deprived of for years. "Mack, always a pleasure to see you. And who is your lovely friend."

"Anna and Talia, this is Mia Turner. She belongs to King."

Both women's eyes lit up. "Did you say 'belongs to King'?"

Mack lifted my wrist and showed them. Of course, I found all of these depraved rules to be shocking as hell and downright offensive, but why these two twigs were flabbergasted was beyond me.

"Wow." Anna practically gasped her words with disdain while looking me over. "I never thought I'd live to see the day."

"King is full of surprises," Mack said. "He's also in the mood to make some trades tonight."

Talia's eyes lit up. "Oh, this *is* going to be a good party. Does he still have that serum?"

Mack nodded. "Yes, it's the last vial."

Of course, I immediately wondered what the hell this serum was. I'd have to ask later.

"And what is he asking for in return?" Anna asked.

"Seems that his tracker found herself with a hole in her body. He'd like yours."

Talia's brown eyes, heavy with smoky eye shadow, lit up. "He's mad. He can't have her. I need her for another acquisition."

Mack's blue eyes exuded charm. "You know King will make it worth your while."

"Mmmm…Do you mean he'll throw you in, too, Mack? I think I might like to have you for a while. I'd treat you better than that bitch Miranda."

The conversation had gone from strange to upsetting. I just couldn't believe that these "civilized people" were standing around, sipping champagne, talking about trading human beings. It was wrong on so many levels.

And you belong to the human pantry. Good job, Mia. Reach high.

"No," Mack said politely, "sadly, I am not on the table tonight. Nor do I ever plan to be. But King knows you've been looking for the services of a Seer. He says he'll loan you one."

What the hell? I looked at Mack. "He can't do that." Maybe these sick people lived by their creepy rules, but I didn't.

Anna smiled wickedly. "My dear Mia, are you his Seer?"

Mack quickly redirected. "Mia is King's special toy. Nothing more. The Seer happens to be a friend of hers."

Suspicion flickered in Anna's and Talia's eyes.

"Fine. Tell King I'll loan him my tracker for two weeks in exchange for the serum. Two weeks. And tell him that she'd better come back alive and in working condition. As for his Seer, tell him to call me. I want to talk about a more permanent arrangement."

Mack nodded his head and placed his palm on my lower back. I had to admit, he did make me feel safe. "As usual, it's been a pleasure."

Anna smiled. "Sure you don't want a little extra pleasure tonight, Mack? I don't fly back to Italy until the morning."

"Perhaps next time. I need to return Mia to King this evening. You know how he is about his toys and punctuality."

Talia rolled her eyes. "Yes. King is a pill. But I'll forgive him because he fucks like a hungry wolf."

"I think he fucks like a silky black panther in a man's skin," said Anna. "Just hearing him growl makes me come."

"You're his toy. What do you think, Mia?" Anna asked. "Wolf or panther?"

The two women stared expectantly, and I was almost too shocked to respond.

I looked at my feet and attempted to hide my revulsion. I hated thinking that King was a part of all this. I loathed the thought that he'd slept with these horrible excuses for human beings and that he'd likely done it because he wanted something from them at one point. *Crap.* I even hated myself for feeling this way. Possessive. Jealous. Petty. King wasn't mine, but a part of me wanted him to be. It was like some primal code of morality radiating deep inside my chest. If I belonged to him, didn't he belong to me?

"I don't know," I said. "He seems like just a man to me." My gaze toggled between the two women. "One with an insatiable thirst for a real woman who can take everything he can dish and give it right back without snapping under his weight. By the way, you should try eating sometime. It could help fill in all those cracks in your souls."

Both women raised their brows.

Mack cleared his throat. "Well, we must be going now. Time to get back to San Francisco."

"It's been a pleasure, Mia," said Anna acerbically.

"Yeah. Fantastic."

Mack hurried me back inside. As soon as we were out of earshot of the women, he stopped me. "Mia, I thought you understood."

"What?" I asked. "Those women were disgusting."

"You're missing the point. They have something we need. And...fuck." He combed his fingers through his golden head of hair. "What was that?"

I looked away, feeling ashamed of myself for losing control.

"Please don't tell me you have feelings for him, Mia."

My eyes snapped to his. "No, I don't."

"Then what the hell was that?"

I shrugged. "Nothing. I just didn't like the way they spoke about King. I didn't like the way they spoke about you, either. We're not animals. We're people."

Mack released a breath toward the ground and shook his head. "It sounded like more than that to me."

"It wasn't."

"Fine." He gripped my shoulders and looked down at me. Funny. It was the way Justin would grab me when he wanted to make a point. "Whatever you do, Mia, don't become emotionally invested in him. He's not that type of person."

"King is the last man on Earth I'd ever feel anything for. He agreed to find my brother. That's it."

He pinched my chin. "I hope you're telling the truth."

"I am." King was a means to an end. And I was, well, his, I supposed. At least in the eyes of the people belonging to this depraved world who thought it was okay to own people.

"Let's get the hell out of here."

"Okay. But I really need to hit the loo." I smiled. "Too much champagne."

Mack walked me down a long hall to a door. "I'll wait here, and hurry the hell up before you start a real fight. With that dress, it's only a matter of time."

"Ha." I entered the bathroom and locked the door behind me.

"Hello, Mia." A sickly, cold hand smothered my scream as my body slammed against the wall.

"Mia?" Mack knocked on the door. "Are you all right?"

Vaughn's beady eyes were an inch from my face. "Tell him you tripped. Tell him you're fine, or I'll fucking gut you like a fish."

That's when I noticed the sharp blade pushing into that spot right beneath my ribs.

Vaughn pressed his entire body against mine like a slithery snake about to constrict its prey. "One jab and I'll puncture your lung. You'll drown in your own blood. Nod if you understand."

I nodded frantically.

"Good. Now tell him." He slid his hand away from my mouth, but kept his body tightly pressed to mine. I wanted to retch. All I saw was red. Everywhere.

I clenched my eyes shut. "I'm fine, Mack. I ju-just tripped. Be out in a sec."

Vaughn pressed his cheek to mine. "Good," he whispered.

I couldn't breathe. I couldn't move.

"I want you to tell King how I touched what was his. You'll tell him how much you liked it."

I intuitively struggled, but he jabbed his knife into my ribs, piercing my skin. His hand landed over my mouth the moment I yelped.

Ironically, all I thought of was how badly the women of the world needed to unite to exterminate all and any rapists. It was the most vile, decrepit display of power one human could exhibit over another. It was a telltale sign that evolution had skipped several generations in a man's bloodline.

But knowing that fact was no help to a woman being confronted by a man like Vaughn who delighted in the unthinkable: murder, rape, buying women like he bought art.

"Might makes right; that's their only real rule," Mack had said.

Vaughn began to gyrate and pump against my tensed body, his hand sliding between the slit at the front of my dress, clumsily searching between my legs.

"Don't fucking move, bitch," he breathed into my ear.

It's okay, I told myself. *It's okay. Everyone who loves you will understand that you'd rather die than let this animal touch you. Justin will understand, too. No one will blame you.*

"I'm not yours, Vaughn. And after you kill me, just know that King will tear you apart, limb from limb."

Vaughn continued to rub against me, breathing heavily. "That's exactly what I want, for him to try anyway."

"Vaughn, you have one point five seconds to remove that hand from Mia, or I will remove it for you."

Vaughn froze and turned his head. He attempted to say the name of the angry man in a black tux standing a mere two feet from us, but that was a half a second too long.

King threw him to the floor, somehow severing Vaughn's arm in the process. Blood gushed from the exposed, raw meat that was now Vaughn's shoulder.

I kept my back plastered to the wall, which provided the only crumb of comfort available to me in this horrific scene. Then I looked at King and, for the first time, saw something within him that truly terrified me. His eyes radiated with savage brutality. He was rage in a suit. Pure violence masked in a man's skin.

"King?" I said.

His eyes flinted as if I'd triggered an awareness in him. He stepped away from Vaughn and drew a breath. And though Vaughn wailed and Mack pounded on the door, everything around us seemed to melt away.

"Are you all right, Miss Turner?" King asked.

I nodded, confused and somewhat awestruck by King's presence. "Yeah. I think so."

He flashed a reassuring smile and tilted his head. "It was never for me. Remember that." His silvery gaze flickered to my wrist.

I stared at him, attempting to decipher his words.

Had he meant the tattoo? I looked at my wrist and then at him. That's when it hit me. How had King gotten here? At the exact moment I needed him, he was there. The bathroom had been locked, and the only two people inside were the monster and me.

I clenched my fists. "How?"

Mack burst through the door, ready to attack. The moment he saw Vaughn wailing in agony, trying to stop his blood from flowing onto the bathroom floor, he froze and grinned. "There's something you don't see every day."

I moved to point to King, but he was gone. Gone. Like a cloud of fog.

My head snapped from side to side as did my eyes.

"Mia?" Mack snapped his fingers in my face. "You okay?"

I looked down at my body. Spatters of blood covered my chest and arms.

"I think so, but...where did he go?" I searched in Mack's blue eyes for the answers.

Mack hesitated before saying, "Let's get you home."

"Okay." I glanced down at the puddle of blood surrounding my feet. Vaughn continued to scream, and that's when I grasped how I enjoyed watching this man suffer. I wanted to see him die. It made me happy to think of a world without him.

Who was I becoming? I'd never been a vengeful person before.

"I'm going to fucking kill you, Miss Turner," Vaughn howled. "I'm going to catch you and pick the flesh from your bones and make King watch. Then I'll do the same to him."

"Enjoy your one arm, asshole." I turned to leave, but a crowd of men in tuxedos had gathered in the doorway. They didn't lift a finger to help Vaughn, but they didn't want to let me pass, either.

Mack began to speak, but I cut him off.

"I'm King's." I showed them my brand.

They quickly moved out of my way, and I knew there was no going back.

I *was* the property of King.

And a dark part of me really liked it.

CHAPTER FOURTEEN

By about one in the morning, Mack got us back on the jet, heading to San Francisco. We didn't talk much during the flight even though I sat in the cockpit, wrapped in a blanket, thankful for the black dress—sans blood—I'd brought with me.

The entire flight, I stared down at the veins and clusters of lights as we flew over towns and cities. I thought of the people tucked in their cozy beds, blind to the existence of 10 Club. Congressmen, CEOs, influential celebrities, I saw them all tonight. 10 Club was like a living, breathing cancer roaming the earth, with a deep, influential reach into our everyday world. I wanted to feel numb or afraid, because I think that's how a normal, rational person might feel, but I didn't. I felt…hungry. Not for food, but for truth. I wanted answers. And I didn't mean from Mack. Not that he would have said much anyway. He was loyal to King, and now I knew that King was loyal to us, too, in some strange way. That's what Mack had meant when he'd said that no one messed with you if you belonged to King. I couldn't deny that it felt like a drug. It instantly turned you from victim to an absolute. Yet, at the same time, I realized how vulnerable I was without King. Tonight, Vaughn had decided to break "the rules" by touching me. It meant that whatever laws 10 Club had, they were subject to being broken just like any law. That got me thinking again about "might makes right." It was the only thing that truly kept me safe: King's ferocious might and his ability to protect what was his from those animals.

How the hell did you get mixed up in this whole thing, Justin? I still couldn't believe it.

When we landed in the dark drizzle at the S.F. airport, Arno was waiting in the SUV just outside the chain-link fence, but I didn't want to go home. I wanted to see King. I wanted to rip myself wide open to the truth. I know, it sounded savage, but that's how I felt. I was knee-deep in this strange world where the rules of civilized men were dead and laws of the physical world—at least the one I knew—meant nothing. I wanted to be armed. I wanted to survive. I wanted to save Justin if there was any hope of it at all.

"I want to see him. Where is he?" I asked Mack before I stepped out onto the Jetway stairs.

Mack shook his head. "He's not going to be pleased about how the party went, Mia. You might want to let him cool off for a day."

"I'm not afraid of him," I said.

"You should be. He gave you specific instructions for the party. You disobeyed him."

"That thing with Vaughn wasn't my fault. He attacked me in the bathroom," I argued.

"Perhaps, yes. But he also told you to keep quiet."

I nodded. "I know." I wondered if I'd done any real damage, but that wouldn't matter. King would only care about the "disobeying" part.

"Go home, Mia. You need to get some rest."

"Don't tell me what I need." Because not even I knew that. But I knew I wanted to see King.

Mack looked into my eyes and smiled with pity. "He's not far. He never is."

"What does that mean?"

He reached for my cheek and stroked it affectionately as if wishing me some sort of luck. "Good night, Mia."

"Good night, Mack."

I got into the SUV with Arno, and we hit the freeway. "Take me to his office, please."

Arno glanced at me in the rearview mirror. "As you like."

The entire drive, I thought about what I might say to King. I wanted to thank him for stopping Vaughn; however, I also needed to draw a line. Because now I fully understood King's world. Weakness would get you killed, and the only thing these people respected was power. That meant I had to be strong. I had to stand up for myself. I had to start with King. Otherwise, I would end up placed in these sorts of dangerous situations over and over again. And some day, King might not be able to save me.

Thirty minutes later, I stood in King's dark empty loft, desperately hoping he'd be there. I knocked on the door to his personal office, but no one answered.

"I am here, Miss Turner." His masculine silhouette emerged from the shadows of the corner just like it had that first night we met. Only tonight, he still wore his tuxedo from earlier.

Suddenly, I couldn't speak. So many questions flooded my mind that they became jumbled in my throat, sounding like an epic fit of stuttering.

King stepped into the light, and I caught a glimpse of his carnally sinful lips. "I am still amazed that my assistant isn't able to speak, answer phones, or," he paused briefly, "follow a simple set of fucking instructions."

I nodded. "True. All true."

"And yet," his eyes washed over my body, "you do know how to make a man do incredibly stupid things. Like lose his arm."

Every girl's aspiration.

King stepped a few feet closer, and I felt the raw, virile energy raging off his body. The room suddenly felt smaller. And hot. *I* suddenly felt smaller and hot.

I took a step back and bumped into the desk.

Be strong, Mia. Stand up to him.

King looked at me expectantly, his beautiful silver eyes drilling right through my soul.

I took a solid breath. "Who are you really, King? How can you vanish into thin air? How can you hurt someone with just a touch? How did you track me to Edinburgh using a stupid tattoo and then just happen to have a suite at the nicest hotel in town?" I could've gone on for an hour with all of my questions, but it was pointless. Everything about King boiled down to two things: he had powerful abilities that defied logic, and he commanded complete control over everything in his world. Except for me. And I wanted to keep it that way.

He rubbed his thumb over the scruffy tip of his chin. "I travel extensively for business, Miss Turner. There's hardly an inch of this world that I haven't touched, but Edinburgh happens to be a frequent hunting ground of mine. As for your other questions, I am just a man. One who's taken an interest in acquiring unique objects and abilities."

"You mean magic?"

"Magic," he scoffed at the word. "We had this conversation already. Magic is a fantasy. It has no basis or foundation in reality. My gifts, as are yours, are real. We merely lack the science and technological sophistication to explain them. Just as cavemen lacked the knowledge to explain gravity. Just as early explorers were baffled when their ships did not sail off the edge of the world."

"So you can make people do things they don't want to do, pop in and out of rooms like a ghost, and tear off a man's limbs with the flick of your finger, and you're saying there's an explanation, but you just don't know what it is?"

He crossed his arms. "I confess I do know quite a bit more than I'm letting on, but many of the objects in my arsenal remain a mystery even to me."

I just didn't buy his story. How could someone dedicate himself to finding these "unique" abilities and objects but lack any interest in them. He was hiding something. But what? "And you're not the least bit interested?"

"I'm interested, but there are only so many hours in a day. I can spend them attempting to unlock the mysteries of the universe, or I can focus on acquiring the tools and power necessary to obtain what I really want."

"Which is?" I asked.

"It is something I've been after for a very long time."

"The Artifact."

"No. The Artifact is simply another tool. What I'm after is far, far more important."

"Which is?" I asked again.

He gave me a look indicating he wasn't going to tell me. Possibly because, as Mack stated, members of 10 Club never wanted their true desires known. Desire meant you had a weakness. Weaknesses could be used against you. And King would never put himself in that position. He'd never admit to desiring anything. Not even me.

Still, what could a man like King really be after? He had wealth, looks, power, and, well, he could call it what he liked, but I called them supernatural powers. He could do things that no regular person could. The only thing my mind came up with was eternal youth or immortality.

"So this...*thing* you're after. Is it why you belong to 10 Club?"

He took a step closer, and I instinctively wanted to take another step back, but the desk blocked my way.

"What I'm looking for," he said in a deep, low voice, "is like searching for a needle in one billion hay stacks—a fucking unicorn. So yes, the club is symbiosis at its finest. I possess abilities and have acquired things people want. In exchange, the members bring me things I need to aid my search."

"You trade with them. Just like you were about to trade me away to those disgusting bitches you screwed."

He laughed, clearly amused. "My standards are infinitely higher than that, Miss Turner. They were merely testing you. So was I."

"Sorry?"

"The party was a test, as was your dress. I rolled you in honey and sent you into the bear's lair."

So that's what the dress was about? "Why would you do that?"

"I wanted to see if you could be trusted. You failed. You disobeyed me yet again, leaving me no alternative but to punish you." He grinned, clearly pleased by the thought of laying his hands on me again.

"Oh my God. You're lying. You knew I wouldn't be able to hold my tongue. You wanted me to screw up so you would have an excuse to 'punish' me."

The vibe inside the dark room turned heavy and hot, like a steam room that instantly made you sweat and want to shed your clothes. My breath became quicker. My skin began to tingle with anticipation. Images of King touching my naked body, pressing against me with his hard frame, kissing me with that seductive mouth bombarded my mind.

This had to be another of his mind games. Didn't it? Yet, more than anything, I want it to be real. "Don't touch me, King."

"Maybe I won't." He spoke quietly. "Maybe I will trade you to Anna and Talia."

"I won't play your depraved game anymore."

"It's not a game, Miss Turner." His voice was deep, seductive, barely above a whisper. "You belong to me. I can do as I please with you."

The twisted little part of me that enjoyed belonging to him delighted in his words, and I hated myself for it.

"*People* aren't things; you can't own them," I murmured. "It doesn't matter what the rules of your degenerate little club say."

He placed his index finger directly under my chin to level me with his gaze, though he didn't have to. I was already crumbling. "Everyone participates of their own free will, Miss Turner. Even you."

"Free will?" I took a shallow breath. "You took advantage of my desperation."

"Yes. And you let me. Because I had something you wanted: the ability to find people. Which makes you no different than me. People use people to get what they want, and you went in with your eyes open."

"Uh-uh. It's not the same, and I had no idea what I was getting into." However, as I said those words, I already knew they weren't entirely true. I felt a sick little rush every time I got near him, even—and God forgive me for it—on that first night.

"But didn't you?" He stepped in, just inches away, and I felt the heat from his supremely masculine body.

I began to tremble with fear, with yearning, with adrenaline. He was like a flame fueled by pure sin that I craved to touch.

"Didn't you know," he slipped his hot hand to the side of my face and threaded his fingers in my hair, "deep down inside, that I was a dangerous man? That, if you made a deal with me, you would have to keep it?" His eyes flashed down to the desk as he bent to my ear. "That I'm a greedy, cruel bastard who gets what he wants?"

Maybe. Still, a part of me wanted to believe that there was a redeeming, good side to him, too. And that part was the reason I felt an attraction. Otherwise, what sort of person did that make me?

There isn't any real good in him. He only protected you because he sees you as an asset.

I sighed inside my head. Maybe King had been right; I was too frightened to take a good look at myself. I was attracted to a man who was evil—*a cruel greedy bastard who gets what he wants*.

"Yes, I knew," I whispered.

"Then why did you take the deal, Mia? What is it that you really wanted from me?" His stubble scraped against my cheek as his husky voice hummed inside my ear, touching my thoughts.

"Help finding Justin." Another half-truth.

My knees began to shake, and I leaned my entire weight back into the desk to keep from falling.

He quietly tisked at me, sounding like a deadly viper hissing its displeasure. "You'll have to lie better than that if you're going to convince anyone, Mia."

He stepped even closer, our bodies barely touching, and I shivered. Being so close to King drew out an animalistic urge that had no rhyme or reason.

"You seem to have all of the answers, King. Why don't you tell me?" I whispered and gripped the edge of the desk behind me.

"I think you secretly crave the dark side of this world. I think it's what brought you here that night. I think it's what draws you to me in this very moment when you know how truly fucked up my world is." He paused and ran his finger along my jaw, triggering another shudder. "Because you know, Mia, how dangerous I am; I could snap your neck in a simple heartbeat."

I turned my face, and we were nose to nose, exchanging the air from our lungs, our lips an inch apart. "Then why don't you, King? Because I'll never be your obedient pet. You'll never control my mind."

He slipped his powerful hands to my waist and pressed his body firmly against mine. His stiff cock pressed into my stomach and sent a flood of scorching hunger spiraling through my body. "I don't need tricks to control your mind when I can control your body." He snaked one arm around the small of my back and pressed himself tighter to me. His warmth, his smell, his hardness were a seductive elixir.

He had to be the devil. He had to be. That was the only explanation that fit everything: his power over me, his strange abilities, his raw sexual energy.

I closed my eyes, wanting to resist the urge to run my hands up his chest, loosen his tie, and unbutton his shirt. I wanted to touch him. I wanted to feel the steely curves of muscles pressed against my naked flesh. I wanted to feel the weight of him on top of me, sweating, digging, and grinding. I wanted to hear the sound of his hard breath and deep primal groans in my ear as he thrust himself inside me.

King nuzzled my cheek, his breath steaming against my face like a bull about to charge. He leaned his chest into me, forcing me to sit on the desk. He pulled his head back and stared deeply into my eyes. I felt lost in the shimmering depths of silvers, grays, and pale blues of his gaze that seemed more like a dark ocean, swimming with mystery, framed by thick black lashes.

His hands moved from my hips to my knees and slowly opened them, hiking up my black dress.

He hit me with the full force of his lips and pushed himself against the juncture between my thighs, reminding me that I'd not worn any undergarments that night.

I nearly fell completely back onto the desk, but braced myself, propping my arms behind me. His lips and tongue were a fiery mess of smooth, soft roughness. He tasted like salt and whisky. He tasted better than any food or drink ever to touch my tongue. He tasted like pure male, pure lust, pure need.

With his one arm pillared at my side, King hovered over my tilted body and cupped the back of my head, smashing our mouths together in a powerful tangle of friction and motion. All I could think of was how I didn't want this. I didn't want this dark, ruthless man that was more like a deadly beast designed to break me. But I couldn't stop what my body wanted.

I thrust against him with my heaving chest and backed him up, breaking the kiss. I sat upright, wanting more than anything to see him, all of him.

Our eyes locked, I slid my hands up his chest and loosened his black bow tie. Then one button, two buttons, three…The look on King's face was intense and carnal, as if he might devour me while I desperately labored to strip him of his clothes.

Buttons finally worked free, I pulled his shirttails from his pants, where I caught the unmistakable outline of his massive cock thrusting against his zipper. He bent his head to mine and kissed me again. I shed his shirt and coat to the floor, leaving him bare from the waist up. He held my head tightly to his mouth, sensually working me with his tongue and full lips while my hands satisfied the urge to explore his body.

Broad shoulders, rounded ridges of well-defined pectoral muscles, arms swelling with thick biceps, every inch of King was lean, hard, menacing muscle. When my hands made their way to his rippled abdomen, I jerked back, wanting to drink him in with my eyes.

That's when I again noticed the intricate tribal collar tattoo covering his collarbone and upper pecs.

I ran my fingers over the design. "What is this?"

"It's nothing." He brushed my hand away and returned to ravaging my mouth. His hands glided behind me and unzipped the back of my sleeveless black dress. He peeled it down, running his hot hands over my shoulders. Again he leaned into me, forcing me to tilt back on the desk so he could access my neck. His mouth slid and sucked and massaged its way down. His arm worked its way around my back and forced me to arch my chest into him.

"Mmmm…No bra," I heard him whisper right before his mouth made contact with my nipple. The sharp suction turned the throbbing ache between my legs into a scorching wave of carnal defeat. There was no going back. I had to give into the rush of wanting something that I shouldn't, into the rush of holding something so volatile and dangerous close to my skin.

"No underwear either," I said. My hands reached for his belt and began unfastening.

"I find that very arousing." His hand journeyed under the hem of my dress and began stroking me with a thick finger. I froze for a moment and groaned, as did he, but then my body quickly answered the urge to rock against his hand.

"That's right," he said when I widened my legs further for him.

Oh my God, the way he touched me was pure sin. I had never wanted a man so badly.

Wait. "Condom," I breathed the word.

King slid his free hand over my tattoo and whispered. "No need for that, Mia." Then his sinful mouth returned to mine.

No need. No need. The thought of protection evaporated from my mind like a wisp of smoke. *Just get him inside me.*

The phone on the desk rang, jarring me for a moment, but there was no stopping the momentum, the burning necessity deep inside that begged for King to take me right there on top of that goddamned desk.

King broke our kiss. "I need to answer that."

"No." I pulled his mouth back down to mine. I would evaporate into nothing if he stopped.

He reached for the phone and held it to his ear, only stopping our frantic kissing and grinding for a moment to say, "Yeah?"

He kissed me some more.

"Fine," he said to whomever it was, then hung up the phone, returning his hand to that heated, throbbing spot between my legs.

I unzipped his pants and gripped him in my hands, savoring the feel of his insane thickness, of his length, of his pulsing, velvety hardness.

Our mouths furiously licked and bit and sucked while I tried to angle the head of his cock to my slick and ready entrance. I was already about to explode. One or two strokes and I'd be done.

Then a tiny thought flickered through my mind. No one called this office. Ever.

"Who was it?" I panted.

"No one."

He rubbed the tip of himself over my sensitive bud and groaned again. "You feel so hot, so warm, so—"

"How can it be no one?" I again panted. My mind didn't want to let it go despite what his hands were doing: Wetting the tip of his large shaft, paving the way for the hard thrust I expected him to deliver.

"No one," he growled.

God, I need this so badly. So badly. Him inside me.

"I can tell you later," he added. "After I punish you."

I froze and looked into his eyes. The raw, primal expression could've been interpreted as lust or possession tinged with anger.

My mind scrambled through the situation and thoughts that conflicted with the physical demands screaming from my body. "Wait. What did you say?"

He smiled like a lusty wolf, unsure if it wanted to fuck its prey or eat it. It reminded me of that night in Edinburgh at the hotel. King had had the exact same look in his eyes. The effect was colder than any bucket of ice water.

"Oh my god." I frantically began pushing his heavy frame off me. "Get off of me. Get off of me."

He glared in silence and then slowly pulled back.

"Is this just some punishment?" I spat.

"Is there any other possible way to interpret this in your mind?"

Oh my god. Oh my god. I started to hyperventilate. "No. I-I guess not."

I quickly pulled up the straps of my dress and hopped from the desk, turning my back to straighten myself out. I guessed he was doing the same.

"I can't believe this," I scorned myself, fumbling with the zipper at the back of my dress. "What was I thinking?"

Don't cry, Mia. Don't cry. But that's what part of me wanted to do. How could I be so stupid? How could I forget who I was dealing with?

"I gave you specific instructions for the party, Mia. You disobeyed me." King zipped up the back of my dress and rested his hands on my bare shoulders. The gesture was thoughtful and intimate, like a husband would do for his wife. How dare he?

"Don't touch me."

He spun me around and gazed into my eyes with a look of confusion. "Why are you so upset?"

"Just leave," I fumed.

"It's my office. And you owe me a punishment."

What a strange reality he lived in. "You're sick. You know that, don't you?" I seethed with disgust.

"Yes, I do. And don't ever think for a moment, Mia, that I won't follow through on my threats. Or that I am capable of feeling anything for anyone."

I lifted my chin, pride welding my words. "You're lying to yourself, King. You feel lots of things: hate, disgust, the need to hurt others and make them suffer. What happened in your life to make you like this?"

He tilted his head, and I expected him to say something cruel, something to deflect my words and reestablish his power over me. Instead, he smiled affectionately and ran his thumb over my bottom lip. "The call was your brother."

My heart stopped. "Huh?"

"Your brother. He has made a deal with me. That's where I was earlier while you were making a fucking mess of things at the party."

I blinked and tried to comprehend. "That was Justin on the phone?"

He nodded yes and waited with what looked like cautious curiosity for my reaction.

"What the hell is wrong with you?" I screamed. "Why didn't you let me speak to him?"

King ran his hands through his now disheveled, thick, black hair. He looked uncomfortable. King was uncomfortable. That never happened.

"Oh no. What? What aren't you telling me?" I asked.

He turned away and went to recover his shirt and jacket from the floor.

"King! I'm talking to you."

He calmly shrugged on his shirt, and as he did, I again noticed the sharp grooves of scar tissue on his back. Yes, something horrible had been done to this man to make him this way.

"What do you want to know? Your brother is alive." He buttoned his shirt. "You should be pleased."

"Where is he? What happened to him?" I asked.

King continued to button.

"Would you turn around and look at me?" I demanded.

King did, but the hard emotion in his eyes was not what I wanted to see. It frightened me.

He cleared his throat. "Your brother doesn't wish to see you."

I pointed to my chest. "Me?"

"Your brother offered me the Artifact in exchange for a clean slate." King's steely, cold eyes met mine. "He wants nothing to do with you, your family, or his past. He's asking me for a new identity, money to live on, and a disappearing act so that anyone searching for him will believe he's dead."

King's words crushed me. That couldn't be right. "Why?"

"Your brother got mixed up with Vaughn. He offered Justin a sizeable payment plus unlimited funding for his work in exchange for a lifelong contract."

"And Justin took the deal?" I couldn't believe it. Justin had never been about money. Ever. He was the least greedy person I'd ever known.

King nodded. "Yes. In addition, Vaughn would get dibs on anything Justin unearthed."

"Why would Justin do that?"

King approached me and placed his hands on my arms. "Justin did not know who he was aligning himself with. But once he found the Artifact and realized it was something powerful, he ran."

"And Justin's team? Why were they killed?"

"I'm sure it was Vaughn's retribution."

"Why would Vaughn's men threaten me to stop looking for Justin?"

"I do not know. Maybe he didn't want to risk Justin receiving help from friends or family members. It's easier to track someone down when they have no resources."

Wouldn't Vaughn have had more luck taking me as leverage? King's guess didn't make sense, but then again, nothing in this strange world did.

"But Justin can't be serious. He can't really mean he never wants to see me again." The tears began to trickle from my eyes.

"I wish I could tell you otherwise, Miss Turner; however, I cannot."

I pinched the bridge of my nose. "I can't believe Justin would do this."

"Maybe your brother is not the man you thought."

"What are you trying to say?" I asked.

"Your brother may not have been aware of who Vaughn really was, but he still agreed to the deal. One that equated to stealing." King held up his hand. "Not that I'm opposed to such activities—after all, one must do what they have to in this world—but your brother was not an innocent child."

"I don't care what he did. He's still my brother, and I love him."

"I am sure you do, but that doesn't change anything."

"I want to see him."

"I cannot do that. I accepted your brother's offer, and I must uphold his terms. This is how things operate in our world."

I pushed King's chest, but it had no impact. "Negotiate new terms," I demanded.

He crossed his thick arms. "No."

"Why not? Because I don't have anything to persuade you with or trade you for?"

He shook his head. "That is not the reason."

"Then tell me! Why not?" I wailed.

He didn't say anything. Instead, he pierced me with his iron gaze.

"You want me to finish what we started on this desk, is that it?" I yelled and felt the dark office fill with energy so heavy that I could barely breathe. "You want me to submit to your punishment to save him?"

He ground his teeth. "I won't deny that the idea of fucking you over that desk makes my cock hard. But your submitting will not change my position."

King was admitting to wanting me? I mean, I knew he did, but he was admitting it.

This was when my brain hit a deep, dark, emotional pothole. King never said or did anything without a reason. He didn't waste a moment of his beautiful, precious time if it did not please him or drive him closer to his ultimate goal, which meant that those sexually explicit words had been said to take the fight from my angry sails. Hadn't they?

I clenched my fists and resisted the bait. "Why won't you talk my brother out of this?"

"Because," he tugged at his crisp white cuffs peeking out from beneath the sleeves of his tuxedo jacket, "your brother does not deserve saving. He's not a good man, nor will he ever be. And I want the Artifact. Therefore my reneging on the deal with your brother simply to appease you serves no purpose. And finally, you will submit to me anyway, Miss Turner. You want to fuck me as badly, if not more, than I want to fuck you. I'm willing to wait—makes life more interesting. Don't you agree?"

Rage sparked my vision. King was the master of mental chess, and he was trying to use sex to get under my skin, to distract me from the real issue, but I couldn't let him. As for his accusations of Justin being unworthy, all I saw was that my brother wanted to find a way out of his mess while insulating his family. If I could get King to see past his greed, then perhaps I could get him to see there was another way. "Haven't you ever cared about anyone or anything, King?"

"Do not be ridiculous, Miss Turner. I care about many things; your brother is simply not one of them."

I laughed bitterly. Again, it was all about getting this Artifact. "Hell, King. I don't know what happened to you, but it must've been bad. I really pity you."

"Have you ever thought for a moment that, perhaps, the reason I am this way is because I once had someone just like your brother in my life?"

It was a confession I hadn't expected from King, but if someone he loved hurt him, it might explain why he was so tainted. "I'm sorry that someone caused you pain. I truly am. But Justin isn't like that. He made a stupid mistake, and now he's about to make another by shutting the door on the people who love him. All I'm asking is to have a discussion with him, to find out if there's another way to resolve the trouble he's in."

King sighed with impatience. "Miss Turner, this is what you are failing to understand. Yes, there is another way. However, it would require making a deal with Vaughn. Is this a path you are willing to go down?"

Shit. Shit. Shit. King was right. If Vaughn was the one Justin needed to hide from, then there were no deals to be made.

"No. But why can't something be done about Vaughn?" I asked.

"As in kill him?"

I looked at King, but didn't respond. He knew what I meant, and he likely knew that I wasn't the sort of person to say those sorts of things out loud. Still, I thought them. Oh, Lord. I thought them.

"It's not so simple. He is a member of 10 Club. Why do you think I left him alive on both occasions?"

I supposed I had wondered why King hadn't killed him. "Don't tell me those people object to murder?"

"Not at all. They simply object to members openly murdering each other. Not to say it doesn't happen all the time, but one must make a superficial effort to respect the laws and cover their tracks. At the moment, I would be the obvious culprit." King pretended to look at his watch and then grabbed his tie. "I am late. I must leave now. You will need to stay with Mack until I return."

"Why do you always do that?"

"Do what?" I watched King make a quick, but perfect knot with his bow tie. I tried not to think about why he was re-dressing himself or how, even now, even after what just happened between us, I still couldn't help looking at the man and feeling something I shouldn't. Perhaps King was right; a part of me was just as dark as him. That part was drawn to him and eventually going to cave to its desires to have him physically.

"Why do you look at that sundial tattoo? What is it?"

He flashed an annoyed look at me. "I'll be back as soon as I can, Miss Turner. And I meant what I said about staying with Mack. Until things are

settled with your brother and Vaughn, you are a
pawn for the taking."

I rubbed my lids with the heels of my palms
"When will you be back?"

King smiled, and it was that charming smile I
now knew he used when he wanted to hide some
dark, sinister thought.

"Hopefully by tomorrow night. I need to meet
with the 10 Club council to discuss Vaughn's
accusations."

"Accusations?"

"He is saying that he rightfully owns you and,
therefore, had every right to touch you."

My stomach twisted in on itself. Obviously, that
was a lie. King had marked me even before we went
to Vaughn. And even so, Vaughn never gave King
the Artifact. There was no "deal."

"What are you going to do?" I asked.

King smiled. This time, it was a genuine one.
"Are you worried for me, Miss Turner?"

I shrugged and looked down at my feet. "Can
you tell Justin I love him and that I don't blame him
for any of this?" The tears began to trickle again.
"And…if he ever gets the chance, we hope he'll
come home."

Even as the words left my lips, I knew that
would be hard unless Vaughn was somehow dealt
with. And from what King had just said, that might
not ever happen unless someone, other than him,
decided to take Vaughn down discreetly.

King nodded and headed for the door.

"Take good care of him, King," I said.

"If your brother delivers the Artifact, he will want for nothing the rest of his life."

Except his family, I thought. But it was better than him being dead.

"Oh, and Miss Turner?" King looked back at me with those hypnotic eyes.

"Yes?"

"You are not off the hook. Remember, I am a man of my word."

I swallowed hard and watched his large, sleek, suited body disappear out the door. King meant that he still wanted to punish me.

"We'll see about that, King."

I would never again make the mistake of giving in to my desire for him.

CHAPTER FIFTEEN

After King left, I took a long, long time to gather myself. After all, I was in no hurry to go anywhere with my broken heart. King would be gone for the next few days, permanently severing my brother from my family while I'd be stuck with Mack, wondering what on earth to say to my parents. Soon, they'd be receiving word that Justin was dead. Dead. And I'd know that wasn't the truth.

"This can't be happening," I muttered.

"I feel like that at least once per day."

I jumped.

Mack. He stood in the doorway looking exhausted. He wore a pair of faded button flies and an army green T-shirt. The ink on his bare meaty biceps and forearms was on display, making him look more like a football player than an ex-military-whatever-slash-pilot-slash-bodyguard.

"Hey," I said and flashed a smile at his tired face.

"Hey." He jerked his messy blond bedhead in my direction and yawned. It had only been about an hour or so since we'd landed at SFO.

"Long time no see." I sighed and passed him, heading for the elevator, where I caught a glimpse of myself in the reflection of the stainless steel doors.

Crap. I tried to smooth out my own bedhead—the one resulting from five frisky minutes with King—before Mack noticed.

"Yeah," Mack said. "Being away from you was so brutal that I decided the only way to cope was sleeping."

That man really liked his sleep. "Sorry. I'm sure you know this wasn't my idea."

"Yes, I know. So…how'd it go? Was he hard on you?"

Oh hell. How could I possibly respond to that? King had been hard on me, but not the way Mack meant. "I guess you could say that."

Mack responded by crinkling his brows, as if to say, "Huh?"

We stepped inside the elevator and rode down in awkward silence. The elevator doors opened, and we stepped outside onto the cold, wet street. At least the drizzle of rain had stopped.

"So," I said. "I guess I should call Becca and warn her we're coming." I started to dig my cell from my handbag.

"You're staying at my place tonight."

I looked at Mack's jetlagged expression. "Your place?"

"Relax," he grumbled. "Don't look so panicked. It was King's suggestion."

"King suggested I sleep at your apartment?" I found that hard to believe.

"I happen to live in a house, Mia. But, yes, this was his suggestion. He said that after your punishment, you might need a little comfort."

Comfort? Punishment? I ran my tongue over my teeth. What did that even mean? If I'd had sex with King, was he implying that Mack would be there to cuddle with me afterwards because King sure the hell wasn't going to do it? Or had King really intended to hurt me and leave me a mess? *What a sick—*

"You okay, Mia?" Mack asked.

I nodded. "Yeah, I'm fine."

"What did he do to you?"

I cleared my throat. "Nothing. He did nothing. I don't want to talk about it."

Mack raised a brow. "Okay."

My cell buzzed in my hand. It was my father. "Dad?" I looked at my watch. It was three in the morning. "What's wrong?"

"It's your mother. She had a stroke."

My body filled with a shock so profound that I couldn't move. "Is she all right?"

"No. She's in a coma." My father's voice quivered.

"Where are you?" I asked. Mack gripped my shoulder, knowing something bad had just happened.

"We're at the St. Francis emergency room."

"I'll be right there," I said.

"Mia," he said, "I remember you took that man's card. The one who came to see us about Justin. I need you to call him and find your brother."

Shit. My brother. "Uh. Okay." I ended the call and looked at Mack. "I need to get a hold of King. It's urgent."

Mack slipped his cell from his pocket and dialed. "Here." He held it out to me. "Leave a message."

"I thought you said that he's never far." Not that I fully understood what that meant.

"He told me if anything came up, this was the best way to reach him tonight."

I grabbed this phone and waited for the beep. "King. It's Mia. You can't let my brother do this. My mom's in the hospital. Shit, King. Tell Justin he can't do this to us. He can't do this to my father. We need him here."

I ended the call, knowing there was little hope of King changing his plans; there wasn't a compassionate bone in that man's body. But I had to try. Didn't I?

Mack and I loaded into his car, which had been parked along the street. It was an expensive-looking, black Mercedes with tinted windows.

"Before you say anything, this is King's car. Mine's in the shop." He smiled. "I drive a Prius. A green one. Because I'm green."

"Oh." I knew he was trying to ease the pain of the moment with a little levity, but he couldn't. I looked ahead at the road and felt Mack's hand cover mine.

"She'll be okay, Mia. Don't worry."

Despite my hopes, I had a feeling deep in my gut that told me she wouldn't be. And if Justin ran away, faking his death, there would be no hope for my father. It would be too much to bear, and I would lose him, too.

"Thanks." I looked at the tattoo on my wrist and slid my palm over it. I wanted to believe that it was like some magical radio that connected me to King, that he might hear my pleas of desperation. *Please, King. Don't do this. Don't.*

For the next few days, Becca, Becca's mother, Teri, and I took turns staying at the hospital with my father, who refused to leave my mother's side. They ran test after test, but they couldn't guarantee that she'd wake up, and if she did, what mental state she'd be in. But I had Internet, and I knew what the statistics said: the longer she stayed in a coma, the lower the chances of her coming out of it. Her chances were now slim to none.

I looked across the hospital bed at my father's sagging face. Knowing my own pain, I couldn't imagine how he felt. "Dad, go home and get some sleep. I'll call you if there's any news."

"I need to stay here—in case she wakes up."

Hearing that was like getting a knife through my heart.

I held back my tears. "Dad, you haven't slept in two days. You're going to make yourself sick." Luckily, he was in fairly good health, but he wasn't indestructible. "Please, Dad? Just for a few hours?" I looked at my watch; it was five in the morning, and he'd stayed up the entire night. "You can come back at noon, and I'll be right here the whole time."

He sighed. "Okay." He slowly rose from the armchair and deposited a kiss on my mother's forehead. "Call me if anything happens."

"I will. I promise."

I stared at my mother's immobile face, tubes running from her mouth. I could only pray now. Not just for her, but for all of us.

"How is she?" King's signature black suit and imposing figure occupied the doorway.

A whoosh of air left my lungs, and I stood. "Where the hell have you been, King?" I said flatly, holding in my rage. He hadn't returned any of my messages, and trust me, I'd left plenty. Mack, who had been camped out in the waiting room, had to cut me off from his phone.

King stepped inside the room and walked over to my mother. He bent his head down as if staring into her eyes; however, her lids were shut tight.

"What are you doing?" I asked.

He kept his nose an inch from hers and ignored me.

I felt the rage bubbling out. "Get away from her," I seethed.

King blinked and lifted his head. "She is fighting."

"What?"

He looked at me, dead serious. "She is fighting to come back, but she's getting tired."

"How do you know that?"

His mouth made a straight line. "I just do."

"You're the devil?" I whispered.

He flashed a peculiar grin that I interpreted to mean my persistence in making this statement amused him.

"Miss Turner, you have the ability to see energy. Do you not?"

I nodded.

"And do I accuse you of being some sort of demon or cursed witch because you were born with a unique gift?"

"No."

"There, you see. Now we can put the issue to rest. And you can see I speak the truth for yourself." He glanced down at my mother. "Look at her."

"I am."

"No. Really look at her." I hadn't thought of using my strange "gift." I guess I hadn't seen any practical use for it other than when hunting for the Artifact.

"What will I see?" I asked.

"Look for yourself, Miss Turner."

I tried to focus my thoughts and relax, but it was impossible. All I saw was my mother's immobile body.

"I can't." I whisked away a tear.

King walked around the bed and turned me toward him. "Your abilities are much greater than you know. Why do you think I chose you?" He stroked the side of my curls, and I felt a flicker of serenity wash over me.

"How do you do that?" I asked.

"Do what?"

"Control my emotions," I explained.

"I do not possess that talent, though I wish I did."

That couldn't be right because King always had a definite influence on me, and those feelings certainly weren't my doing. No. Not possible.

"Perhaps I could persuade you to be more civil if I did." He flashed that charming smile, and I knew he was hiding what he really wanted to say, which could've been anything ranging from "please, be less bitchy" to "be more obedient." I didn't know. "Now, Miss Turner, take another look."

I turned my head and settled my mind on my mother. The colors instantly popped. Greens and blues swirled all over her body.

"What do the colors mean?" I asked, leaning closer to her, completely in awe.

"Red is generally pain, which is why you see it when someone is murdered. Black is death—generally, a painless one. Green is life."

"And blue?" I asked.

"Blue is sorrow."

I looked away and began to cry. I didn't care if King thought me weak for it.

He pulled me into his warm body, but I didn't want comfort from him. Not when I knew he'd be the nail in my father's coffin. Despite that, when he stroked the back of my hair, I began to feel like nothing could ever hurt me. Not when I was wrapped in King's arms.

"The blue is a good sign," he said. "It means she is aware of what is happening to her. It means that she continues to hold on to this world."

I slid my arms underneath his suit jacket. The warmth of his body felt more like a soothing current of tranquility. I nuzzled my face into his broad chest and let my lungs fill freely with air for the first time in two days. I blew it out, clinging to him, wondering how a man so dark and cold could bring me so much peace. Maybe hidden deep down inside, underneath all those scars and greed, was good. Genuine good. But that would be impossible.

I opened my eyes and looked at my mother again. *If only Justin were here, I think I could handle whatever came next.*

Justin. I had completely forgotten.

I pulled back and looked up at King's masculine, ethereally beautiful face.

When his gaze met mine, I saw angry reds and deep dark blues. The colors didn't simply swirl over his skin, but circled his entire body like a violent tornado that moved so quickly the colors transformed to purple. And as strange as I knew it sounded, I could feel the suffering inside him. I was there, inside his head, experiencing the pain with him. Only, I had no understanding of what caused it.

The pain's intensity became too much, and I pushed away from him. "Oh, God."

He didn't meet my startled gaze.

"King?" I held my hands over my mouth.

He held out his hand, cautioning me not to speak. But even if I could, what would I say? What could I say? This man was in an extraordinary amount of pain.

I held my breath and continued to stare at him. Part of me felt horrified, and part of me felt deep pity.

The tears continued to stream down my face, but now it was because I felt so helpless. I couldn't help my mother or my brother, and I couldn't help King.

"Why are you crying?" King asked.

I looked at him and wished I could articulate the profound sympathy I felt. But words would never measure up.

I placed my hand on his rough cheek and stared into his heavenly eyes, willing him to see the sincerity behind them. "I'm sorry."

"For what?"

"For whatever was done to make you this way. No one should have to live like that. No one."

He slid his hand gently over mine and nuzzled my palm.

Through the connection we had, I still tasted his pain. I tasted the anger and rage coursing through his blackened heart, too.

He kissed my palm and moved it from his face, but I didn't want to stop looking at him. I wanted him to know that I saw everything and that he wasn't beyond redemption or salvation. No one was.

"Kiss me," I asked.

"Why?"

Because underneath his broken, twisted, sorrow-filled soul, I'd seen something real and gentle that made me want him. Perhaps, now more than ever—a thought I couldn't bring myself to say aloud, but I couldn't deny. "Because I want you to."

Slowly, he slid his hand around the base of my neck and up to the back of my head, leaving a trail of heat over every inch of skin where we'd made contact. Eyes locked to mine, he bent his head to my mouth. When our lips met, it felt like so much more than a simple kiss. I felt lost in him, his darkness, his need to end whatever agony existed within.

I jerked back and looked at him. *The pain.* I recognized it. Its darkness and bitterness. Its terrible weight.

I held my hands over my mouth again, realizing that the night he'd "punished" me in Edinburgh wasn't some sadistic quest to hurt me; King had simply shared himself with me. *That* had been his "pleasure," allowing his cold, dark, and lonely heart the chance to feel a connection with someone.

With me.

"And now you see, Miss Turner, I *am* a monster."

"Monster?" That's not at all what I saw. I saw someone in desperate need of compassion.

I shook my head. "No. I see a very beautiful man who was hurt."

He glanced at his feet, clearly contemplating my words.

Then, as if he'd come to some sort of conclusion, he stepped back, withdrawing emotionally. The colors swirling over the surface of his skin evaporated. He shut me out.

He straightened his black tie and cleared his throat. "I, uh…" His head snapped up. "I got your messages and spoke to your brother."

"You did?"

"Yes. But," he held up his hand, "he confessed that he is still working with Vaughn."

"Shit. No. He can't be."

King nodded. "Yes. In fact, your brother was about to lure me into a trap when I told him of your mother."

Dammit. Justin, why? Why?

"I explained to him that if he wanted to come home and get his life back, then he would have to work with me. He would have to betray Vaughn and trust me."

I tried to hide my shock, but I couldn't. King had changed his mind. For me. I couldn't help but wonder why. Was there hope for that cold heart of his, yet?

"And?"

King nodded reluctantly. "He agreed."

"What does that mean?" I asked.

"It means that your brother will pretend to set me up. We will meet, he will bring the Artifact, and Vaughn and his men will be waiting for me."

"But you'll be prepared?" I asked.

King nodded yes.

I didn't know what to say. This was a risk, and King was taking it for me. It made me seriously begin to question the lens through which I'd seen him.

"What about 10 Club?" I asked.

"They will know it was me."

"What will they do?"

"After I have the Artifact, there is nothing they can do that will be of any importance to me."

"What will it do for you?" I was suddenly terrified; King's one hope in this world was to end his suffering.

"It has the power to make things right for me."

"Revenge?"

"No, my dear Miss Turner. Something better than that."

My mind spun with horrible, horrible thoughts. To a man like King, what could be better than revenge when someone had caused him so much pain?

King looked at his wrist, this time not bothering to hide the fact he was looking at his tattoo. "I must be off."

Oh my god. My mind couldn't let go of this. What was King really after if not revenge? Death? He didn't need anything special for that. A goddamned gun or some pills would do the job. No. He was after something else, but what?

"When will you be back?"

He smiled—a real one. "Miss Turner, I do believe you are worried about me."

"Maybe. When?"

"If all goes well, I will see you in the morning."

"And Justin?"

"He will be free. As will we all."

"Wait! What are you going to do, King?"

But King wasn't going to answer. He turned and walked right into Becca.

"Oh, crap! I'm so sorry." She stared up at him, looking like she'd just seen Elvis.

He extended his hand. "Becca, it's a pleasure to see you again."

She shook his hand and practically drooled over it. "Nice…to…see…you again, too."

King raised his brows. "Well, I must be off." He dipped his head. "Miss Turner, I hope your mother pulls through."

"Goodnight, umm…" Becca seemed to forget his name.

"King." He flashed a smile at her.

"Is that your first name or your last?" Becca blurted out like a dumb groupie.

Funny, I thought. I'd never asked him that myself. In fact, the question had never crossed my mind.

King gave us one of his charming smiles. "Who said it was either?" He disappeared, leaving us with our churning minds.

Becca turned to me. "His middle name, I guess?"

"Yeah, I guess." Not like there was another option, right?

"Mia?" My mother's faint voice caught my attention.

"Oh my god!" I jumped to her side. "Mom, oh my god. Mom?" I looked at Becca. "Go get the nurse, and call my dad."

Becca bolted from the room, and I sank down next to my mother. "Can you hear me okay? How do you feel?"

I noticed she had pulled the tubes from her mouth on her own. How could we have stood there and not noticed?

My mother kept her eyes closed, but she smiled. "I feel like...well, horrible, actually. But it's good to be back."

I dropped my head to her chest and sobbed.

"Where is the man?" she asked.

"What man?"

"That man in black. He was just here."

I blinked and swallowed the flood of emotions. "You mean King?" I asked.

"Yes. The nice man who brought me back. Where is he?"

I balled uncontrollably. "He left, Mom. He left to go get Justin."

She smiled. "Oh, good. I miss my baby boy."

"So do I, Mom. So do I."

⁂

Later that day, after running a multitude of tests, life spread its wings of hope once again. The doctor confirmed that the road to recovery for my mother would be long, but her faculties were intact, and that was all I could ever ask for.

When my father showed up, his eyes red with tears, he was unable to speak the moment he spotted my mom alert and talking. Then he literally collapsed to the floor. Luckily, the nurse had been standing nearby and brought him around quickly. There was no damage to him from the fall, but I would never forget the image of seeing the man so overwhelmed with joy that he actually fainted.

The rest of the day was spent calling everyone and sharing the miraculous news. Yes, it truly was a miracle. And I had only one person to thank for it: King.

How he'd done it, I didn't know, and I wasn't going to ask. Because this time, he was right; you could spin your wheels asking questions, or you could choose to focus on what really mattered to you. I had her back, and I couldn't begin to express the gratitude I felt toward him; there simply weren't enough words.

"Did I miss all the fun?" said a familiar voice.

I couldn't believe my eyes. In fact, I didn't.

"What?" Justin smiled at me with that dopey grin.

It couldn't be. It couldn't. It was…

"Justin!" I ran and threw myself into his arms. I hugged him so tightly that he grunted. And I wasn't about to let go. He was warm and alive and in one piece. My baby brother—my best friend was really there. Yet again, I began to sob uncontrollably, feeling like an enormous, horrible burden had been lifted from my shoulders.

"Mia, glad to see you, too."

Still bawling, I looked at him and squeezed his cheeks between my palms. I drank in his green eyes and sandy blond hair. "I have never felt so relieved in my life."

"Me too." He flashed a glance at my mother, who was now sleeping. "King told me the good news. How is she?"

"Fine. She's fine. Dad just went down to the cafeteria. He'll be right back." I grabbed both his hands and held them between mine. "Are you okay?"

"Yeah, I'm okay."

He had no possible understanding of how happy I was to hear him speak and say those words.

"And Vaughn? What happened?" I whispered.

"I don't know, Mia."

"What do you mean?"

"I showed up to the empty apartment in London with the Artifact. But King changed the plans on me at the last minute. He called my cell, said to leave the Artifact there, and get on the first plane home."

"What? So where is he?" An ugly knot formed in my stomach.

"I don't know, Mia. But I'm sure he took care of things."

What if he didn't? What if something went wrong?

Are you trying to ruin the moment? King had said he expected to be back in the morning, so it wasn't time to worry just yet.

Then why do I feel worried?

I shook my head. "I can't believe you're really here." I grabbed Justin again and hugged him tightly.

"Justin?" my mother called out. I released my death grip on him and walked over to the bed, holding his hand tightly.

"I'm home, Mom," Justin said. "I'm home."

EPILOGUE

Two Weeks Later.

After Justin's return, I continued to show up at King's office every morning at six a.m., hoping and praying that King would show. But he didn't. At least, not during the few hours I hung around until I had to go to the hospital to see my mother. Nor did he show up at six or call at 6:02 p.m. when I returned to his loft. And, as if that wasn't bad enough, Mack and Arno were nowhere to be found, either.

It was as if King and his men had disappeared off the face of the planet. When I tried to speak to Justin about that night or his deal with Vaughn that had started the entire mess, he broke down and cried. He said he'd never forgive himself for what he'd done to his team. He insisted he'd told me everything about that night he was supposed to have met with King.

By the fourteenth day, I had to start facing facts. Something had gone terribly wrong. Had 10 Club taken King? Or had Vaughn gotten a hold of him? If so, did that mean Vaughn would be coming after me, too? I didn't know. And where the hell had Mack and Arno disappeared to?

Then there was the question of my life. Justin and I were now both crashing at my parents', and I needed to find a paying job. I couldn't sponge forever. But then…what about my deal with King?

And where the hell is he?

I was at my wits' end with worry; however, the only options were to go to L.A. and try to get a meeting with Vaughn or wait. And considering that Vaughn wanted to pick the flesh from my bones, that meant wait. For how long, I didn't know.

6:02 p.m. Another no show.

"Dammit, King. Where the hell are you?" I slammed my fist on the desk, and the pen holder tipped over, dumping its contents to the floor. I got down on my hands and knees to pick up the mess. I gathered the pencils and pens in my hand, thinking how silly it was that they were even there to begin with. Not like anyone ever called to leave a message.

I reached for the last stray pencil all the way underneath the desk, and that's when I saw the envelope taped to the bottom of the middle drawer.

I frantically peeled it off and opened it. Inside were a key and an index card with an address in SOMA, a neighborhood not too far from the loft. I flipped the card over, and on the back was King's mark—the letter "K"–and the number ninety-two. Nothing else.

Had he meant for me to find this? No one else sat at this desk, and it wasn't like King to do anything without a purpose to it.

I scrambled outside and hopped into a cab, hoping and praying that whatever this place was, it would give me some answers.

I gripped the key tightly in my hand and then looked at it. *Crap.* Who was I kidding? It's not like I'd find a secret treasure map leading to his location.

When the cab pulled up to the warehouse overlooking the bay, I got out and stood there, staring at the enormous three-story building about a football field long. What was this place? The vibe was beyond ominous, like it radiated a dark, malicious energy that warned you off. I relaxed my eyes and saw nothing but reds and blacks swirling all around the exterior.

"What is this place, King?" I whispered.

Whatever it was, I had to go inside. I had to. Because if I was right, King wanted me to come here. Perhaps he'd anticipated something going wrong.

But why send me to a place that feels like the edge of hell?

I slipped the key in the lock and prayed.

To Be Continued…

NOTE FROM THE AUTHOR:

Hi All!

I hope you enjoyed Part 1 of the King Trilogy. If you did, I SOOOO appreciate your reviews, emails, Tweets, and Facebook notes! I'm especially curious to hear everyone's guesses as to who our mystery man, King, truly is! Good? Evil? Elvis? (He's the king, get it?) Human? Nonhuman? Hmmm...

By the way, if you're looking for more, you'll be happy to know that Part 2, KING FOR A DAY, is available now! And if you'd like to learn more about King, Mia, Mack, and Arno, including seeing some pics of them and the places in the book, or if you'd like to score some free bookmarks, stop by my webpage (MimiJean.net).

Also, if you're into snarky humor with lots of twists, keep an eye out for my new Contemporary Romance series, The Happy Pants Café, or check out my Accidentally Yours Series! (*Accidentally...Over?*, the series finale, is almost here!! Woohoo!)

HAPPY READING!

Mimi Jean

ACKNOWLEDGEMENTS

I am sure that everyone is tired of hearing me say it, but THANK you to my beta readers! (Vicki, Kylie Gilmore, Nana, and Kim.) You ladies rock!

And I can't forget my dudes, Javi, Seb, and Stef for always pitching in. I know I work too much, but it's always for you!

KING FOR A DAY
(Book 2 of the King Trilogy)

AVAILABLE NOW!

King is not who she thought. She wasn't even close.

When Mia Turner's life becomes tethered to a mysterious billionaire who she swears is the devil himself, she knows she must find a way to break free. It doesn't matter if everything about him—those sinful lips, those pale gray eyes, that perfect male body—keeps her awake at night, restless for him. She has to get away.

But when this man, known simply as King, disappears without a trace, Mia will discover she's not home free. Because the only thing keeping her safe from King's ruthless, depraved, power-hungry social circle had been him.

To live, Mia must not only find King, but conceal his absence and walk a mile in the evil man's twisted, cruel shoes. What she discovers will leave her more terrified and her heart more conflicted than she ever imagined.

King is not who she thought. She wasn't even close.

BUY LINKS CAN BE FOUND AT:
MimiJean.net/king_trilogy_books.html

KING OF ME

(Book 3 of the King Trilogy)

Coming Late 2014!

Don't miss New Release updates! Sign up for Mimi Jean's mailing list:

MimiJean.net

FATE BOOK

(FATE BOOK 2, Coming late 2014)

Dakota Dane is about to tell a lie she'll wish she hadn't. Because her lie is dangerous, sexy, and just showed up on campus, angry as hell and looking for her…

Ugly duckling Dakota Dane has a new boyfriend. He's male-model gorgeous, built to perfection, wealthy, and smart. He is also a lie. As in, 100% fabricated. Does it matter that Dakota has a perfectly good reason for making him up? Not really. Not when Dakota's made-up boyfriend shows up in the flesh.

So is she crazy? All signs point to maybe. But the walking, talking enigma with the deadly vibe isn't about to give her any answers or let her out of his sight. And with college just around the corner, Dakota fears her dreams of a bright future have just collided with a dark rabbit hole…

EXCERPT FROM FATE BOOK

Lord. Whoever had been on the other end of that phone was coming to my room. I had to get out of there. Because as much as I loved believing in miracles, those didn't exist, which meant this guy was some psychopathic stalker, some frigging lunatic who'd convinced everyone he was my boyfriend.

I slipped from the covers and immediately had to brace myself on the edge of the hospital bed. My head pulsed with painful, dizzying jabs. I slowly stood upright and willed myself steady. My ribs and hip were sore, but I'd survive. That was, if I got the heck out of there.

I blew out a breath and wobbled to the clear plastic bag with my belongings hanging on the wall. I had to find my mother. I had to warn her. What if this guy showed up and tried something?

I slipped on my jeans, sweatshirt, and sneakers, not bothering with the other stuff. I grabbed my phone and purse and tiptoed to the door.

I poked my head out, hoping to spot my mother doing rounds, but instead I saw—

The breath whooshed from my lungs. *Santiago?*

Cue slow motion and avalanche of conflicting, irrational thoughts accompanied by an imminent panic attack.

My stomach and heart squeezed into a brick and then dropped through the center of my body.

Lord, help me.

Because the man I'd invented—correction—the *gorgeous* man I'd stolen a picture of, stood twenty feet away, speaking to my mother, wearing low-slung faded jeans and a fitted white, button-down shirt.

I stared in wonderment while my eyes infused with his image and branded itself on my brain. He was lust, rock star, tough guy, jock, Prince Charming, and misfit rolled into one dangerous, rugged, well-groomed package. He sent my female brain into a tailspin.

I've lost my mind. That gorgeous man is not standing there. That's not possible!

I willed my heavy feet to move, but my eyes remained glued to him. He was tall—around six three or six four—and, just like in his photo, built like a lean, mean predatory animal with broad shoulders and powerful-looking…everything. Especially those arms. And those legs. And those…*yep. Everything.* To boot, he stood with the sort of confidence that gave me the distinct impression he really might be deadly. And ate his meat raw. Possibly still squealing.

Santiago, who towered over my mother, leaned down and hugged her. Then my mother said something, and they laughed like old friends.

What? He hugged my mother? What was happening? Did she know him? Was the universe punishing me for lying? If it was, it was totally working. I'd never, ever lie again. *This time, I mean it, Santa.*

For Pics and BUY LINKS:

MimiJean.net/fate_book.html

COMING IN AUGUST, 2014!

The Accidentally Yours Series Finale!

Excerpt of ACCIDENTALLY…OVER?

Prologue

Death is trying to seduce me.

I always suspected he would come for me after I survived the accident, and now there's no doubt. And death isn't some ominous creature that carries a bloody scythe, his face obscured by a black cloak, his spindly fingers protruding from the cuff of his dripping sleeve as he enters your dinner party, points to your plates, and declares in a gravelly voice, "You're all dead. It was the canned salmon." Oh no. This is no snarky Brit skit, and he's no monster.

Death is a sex god.

He's tall, built from indestructible solid bricks of muscle. His cheekbones are chiseled works of art, and his full, sensual lips are meant for doing anything but killing. Like I said, sex god.

How do I know this? He's been watching me, whispering in my ear while I sleep, quietly hiding in the shadows while I eat, while I work, while I shower.

So for once, I'm turning the tables.

I follow the sound of his footsteps through my beach cottage, out my back porch, and then pick up his large footprints in the sand. I crouch behind the tall, dry grass blanketing the massive sand dune. The crashing waves mask the sound of my thumping heart and heavy, frantic breaths. I'm sweating like mad as the tropical morning sun beats down on my back, and I spot my stalker splashing in the waves.

He stands, and I can barely breathe when I look at him.

Though he's nearly transparent, the outline of his naked body glistens with drops of ocean water reflected by the sun. I've never seen a more beautiful man. Shoulders that span the width of two normal-sized men, powerful arms and legs that make me wonder if he's not actually carved from rock or molded from steel, and incredibly sculpted…jeez, everything. There's not an inch on this beast—not a neck, an ab, not a pec or a thigh—that isn't constructed from potent, lethal-looking muscle. Well, except his hair. Though I can't see the color, it's beautifully thick and falls to his shoulders. I imagine it's a warm shade of brown, streaked with reds and golds. Because he's utterly beautiful, and that's the kind of hair a beautiful man would have. Yes, he's a god, not the bringer of death. And I can't help but wonder why he's made that way. Is it so that when he comes for me, there'll be some sort of consolation—getting to see his face? I don't know, but I'm not ready to see it yet. I want to live. I want to grow old. I want to fall in love. Just once before my time is up.

Yet somehow, I want him, too. Why? That's gotta mean I'm *loca*, right?

My eyes study every poetic detail of this "man," hoping to find answers. But there's nothing. Nothing that will help save me from him.

Suddenly, I see his chin lift, and his head turns in my direction.

Can he see me? *Oh my God. He's coming right for me.*

I bolt from my hiding place and make a run for it. I know if I make it to my house, I'll manage to lock the doors, but that won't stop him. There is nowhere to hide from death, but I run anyway.

I make it to my back porch and reach for the door, but I slip on something. *Shit. Really? A banana peel?*

My body crashes to the hard cement. My head cracks on the sharp edge of the porch's step, and I can't move. All I feel is my beating heart and heaving lungs, burning with fear.

"Dammit, woman. Why the hell do you always run from me?" His deep, melodic voice washes over me, and I love how it soothes my soul.

I look up and try to focus my eyes, but he's difficult to make out. His dripping hair catches only a few rays of morning sunlight.

"You're so beautiful," I croak. "But I changed my mind; I don't want to die. Please don't take me away."

I feel his warm hand brush against my cheek. "I am trying to save you, Ashli. Why won't you let me?"

Why does he say that? Why is he lying to me? It doesn't matter now, because I'm already dying. The darkness begins to swallow me.

"Shit!" I roll from my bed and fall to the floor with a thump.

Sonofabitch! Why do I keep having these dreams?

BUY LINKS CAN BE FOUND AT:

MimiJean.net

ABOUT THE AUTHOR

 When San Francisco native Mimi Jean went on an adventure as an exchange student to Mexico City, she never imagined the journey would lead to writing Romance. But one MBA, one sexy Mexican husband, and two rowdy kids later, Mimi would trade in 15 years of corporate life for vampires, deities, and snarky humor.

She continues to hope that her books will inspire a leather pants comeback (for men) and that she might make you laugh when you need it most.

She also enjoys interacting with her fans (especially if they're batshit crazy). You can always find her chatting away on Facebook, Twitter, or saying many naughty words on her show MAN CANDY on Radioslot.com!

You can learn more at:
MimiJean.net
Twitter.com/MimiJeanRomance
Facebook.com/MimiJeanPamfiloff
mailto: mimi@mimijean.net

CPSIA information can be obtained at www.ICGtesting.com
Printed in the USA
LVOW12s0052110614

389518LV00016B/230/P